HELEN GRAY

COMPLEX CONSPIRACY

HELEN GRAY

Ozark Hills Homicide, Book 1

ISBN: 978-1952661204

Chapter 1

Erin Stuart ran a final glance over the front office of the vision center, making sure everything was in order before leaving for the day. This optometry practice in Springfield, Missouri, was her private world, one that had taken years of hard work to achieve.

She picked up her purse, adjusted the air conditioning for overnight and turned off the light. "Okay, Mom, I'm ready to go now."

Her mother, who did not drive because of her blindness, had been delivered by her husband in time to be the last appointment of the day. Now that her eye exam had been completed and no sign of infection or problems found, Erin would take her home. Her assistant, Lydia Carmichael, had already left for the day.

Erin had a small house of her own here in Springfield, but she split her nights between it and the home of her elderly parents, spending as much time with them as she could without slighting her business. They lived in the small town of Ozark, located between Springfield and Branson.

Verna stood from the chair where she had sat in the waiting room while Erin prepared to leave. Moving her white cane in a left to right arc roughly the distance from

5

shoulder to shoulder, she approached the doorway, her progress practiced and competent. Verna had an independent streak that made her able to cope with her blindness like everything else she did, relying as little as possible on her husband and daughter.

That was good, but it didn't mean Erin wouldn't look after her parents. After years of wanting children and not having them, Erin had been born when her mother was thirty-nine years old. Their only child, they had doted on her—still did—and done everything they could for her.

When Erin was in junior high, her mother's diabetes had become so severe that it had cost Verna her eyesight. Erin had become her Seeing Eye dog in the beginning and been by her side through learning to use her white cane and how to function in her dark world. Because of her diabetes and concern about infections, Erin monitored Mom's vision very closely.

Outside in the hallway, the mall bustled with activity. Parents gripped the hands of small children and pushed strollers with babies, while young couples strolled hand in hand, enjoying the refuge of the mall's air conditioning.

When Erin and Verna exited the building, the sweltering mid-July air blasted them, still beating down on the parking lot in rays that felt like laser beams. Erin's lightweight cotton slacks and top that had felt good inside the building now felt heavy and suffocating.

Verna lifted her face, frowning. "I hope your car isn't far—and that your air conditioner cools quick. This pavement is hot enough to fry my feet."

A young woman approached from the sidewalk, extending a flyer. Campaigners had been flocking to the mall since the beginning of election primaries. "Hello, ladies," she greeted them brightly. "I hope you'll help us reelect our state senator, Ray Fielder."

Verna smiled as Erin accepted the campaign flyer. "You're a very devoted supporter to be out campaigning in this heat. I hope you'll get inside soon and have something cold to drink."

"I will." The woman smiled, turned and headed toward the mall entrance.

Erin stepped next to her mother and extended her forearm. "Let's get into the car."

Needing no prodding, Verna placed her hand on Erin's arm and matched her quick pace to the vehicle, their heels clacking on the asphalt. As Erin opened the car door, a shout from behind them made her whip around.

"Stop!"

The mall security guard dashed out the door in pursuit of a young man.

Fleeing across the lot, the young man looked back over his shoulder, causing him to veer slightly off course, directly toward Erin and her mother.

Reacting quickly, Erin grabbed Verna's hand, shoved her inside the car and slammed the door. Then she whirled to circle the vehicle, digging in her purse for her keys as she ran. And the world exploded.

Erin screamed as she and the fleeing man crashed to the pavement. Her purse sailed across the parking lot, the contents strewing from it.

The young man scrambled to his feet, looked around frantically for a couple of seconds and then took off again as the security guard crossed the parking lot in hot pursuit.

The guard paused next to Erin, his gaze scanning her quickly.

"I'm fine," she shouted, waving him away. "Go after him."

He continued the chase, but the moment's hesitation had given the young man the seconds needed to regain his momentum.

Erin crawled across the hot asphalt, retrieved her purse and began scooping the strewn items back into it. As she finished and pushed to her feet, clutching her keys and purse, the guard returned.

"Are you okay, Ma'am?" His voice held an edge, but was of a baritone quality pleasing to the ear.

Erin scrutinized his face, staring into gleaming dark eyes filled with depths she couldn't decipher. A little over six feet tall. Well-toned muscles. Nearly black hair. Hard features. He wore standard cop attire, a dark blue uniform that emphasized taut muscles, and struck her as being maybe two or three years older than her thirty-two years. Anger glinted from those dark eyes that scrutinized her in return.

Frown lines creased her forehead. "I'm okay. Are you new? I don't remember seeing you around. Did Charlie quit his job?" Charlie was the day guard who always greeted her in a friendly manner.

"I was just transferred here this week to cover for him while he's off for some kind of surgery. He should be back in a few weeks."

Erin blinked. Shifted her gaze to where the man's escapee had leaped into a car and was gunning it out of the parking lot. "I'm sorry he got away. What was the problem?"

~

Miles Jarrett had responded to a burglar alarm from a jewelry store, raced down the hall to spot a young man running away, and chased the guy. Having him escape was frustrating.

Behind the woman who had been mowed down by the thief, the car door came partially open. "I'm cooking in here, Erin," an older woman yelled from inside the vehicle.

The honey-blond woman whipped her head around. She was striking, he noted uncharacteristically.

"I'm coming, Mother," she said without taking her eyes off him. "I have to go. Hope you catch your guy."

Miles watched her round the white Camaro, scoot inside and drive away. She was familiar, but he couldn't place her.

And she certainly hadn't done anything to warrant detaining her.

He returned to the jewelry store, interviewed the owner and took notes for a report. Then he went to the security office of the retail complex, located around the corner from the flea market, mixed impressions tumbling around in his head. Knowing he had to get his head back onto business, he pulled out his phone and dialed his superior.

"Miles here," he said when Jed Parker answered. "There was a smash and grab at the jewelry shop. The thief escaped, but I got a look at him. I'll scan through some mug shots and see if I can recognize the guy. I checked for prints around the shop window he broke and had the shop owner determine what's missing from his display. As for our main mission here, I don't have any solid leads yet."

The third largest city in Missouri, Springfield boasted the nicknames Queen City of the Ozarks and Birthplace of Route 66. In contrast, Branson, about forty miles to the south, only had a resident population of a little over ten thousand but was one of the leading entertainment capitals of the nation, featuring live music and family entertainment. The summer tourist season was currently at its height, so traffic was heavy between the towns. In addition to tourists traveling to the live theater shows and other attractions, a lot of people commuted back and forth between the towns to work.

It was too bad that, along with the pleasant activities of the area, there were unpleasant ones. Meth had been around a long time, and cocaine was getting bigger. Sources had alerted the agency that drug buyers were picking up drugs hidden in products at the flea market. Housed in a large section of the mall, nearly a hundred booths occupied it. The DEA's problem was determining which marketers were handling the drugs. Miles had been placed undercover here to watch and identify the culprits and learn the identity of the operation's kingpin.

After ending the call, Miles began one of the rounds that were part of the regular security guard's routine. Sight of the vision center located down the hallway from the flea market made him think of the woman who had collided with his thief in the parking lot. Yes, now he recalled seeing her exit that shop more than once.

The first time she had caught his eye, he had merely assumed she was a patient, but when he saw her again, he had wondered if she worked there, or if she could possibly be the eye doctor.

Always professionally dressed, he now deduced that she *was* the doctor. About five foot three or four, the things about her that had struck him were the brightness of her chocolate brown eyes and the lushness of that honey-blond hair that she pulled back into a casual ponytail with the upper part, leaving the lower portion draping over her shoulders. And there was an impressive air of confidence with which she carried herself.

Suddenly it occurred to him how convenient her shop's location was to the flea market area.

Did the woman have any idea what was going on right around her? If she did, would she care? Could she possibly be involved?

Miles pushed the questions aside. He had to concentrate on his job. The drug operation had to be shut down before more violence erupted. There had already been too many deaths related to the use or dealing of those drugs.

~

Twenty minutes later, Erin delivered her mother to the house where her parents had raised her. Everett, who managed to look after his wife and himself quite well for a seventy-five-year-old retiree, had a pot of potato soup and a pan of cornbread ready to put on the table. Verna was five years younger and did much of the cooking, but her housekeeping abilities had limits. Erin owed them so much. They had been loving and supportive parents. Now she had to support them, take care of them, stay with them as much as she could.

Her mother's blindness had been an inspiration to Erin, but her parents' entire lives had motivated her. A humble pastor and wife, they had been poor materially, but had always given sacrificially of themselves and whatever they had. By the time Erin was seventeen, she had known that God meant for her to do whatever it took to become a doctor in the field of eye care. It had been a long journey, years of schooling that amassed a mountain of student loan debt, but she had reached her goal. Her private practice, established two years ago after working for another organization for four years, was her world.

So what if she had already passed that magical age that people in her world considered past the walking-the-aisle phase. It couldn't be changed. She was content, married to her job.

"If you'll give me your grocery list, I'll shop after work tomorrow for both of us," she told her dad, giving him a hug. "But I need to get back to Springfield now."

Everett's brown eyes narrowed beneath a crown of white hair. "You mean you're not staying?"

"I have laundry waiting for me, so I need to sleep at my own place tonight."

He rolled his eyes. "You can't even eat with us?"

She grimaced, feeling guilty. "I really need to get home."

"And you're not fond of potato soup. Okay, do what you think best. You look after us, but almost too good. You need to stop working so hard and spend more time on yourself."

Erin almost winced, but forced the expression into a weak smile. "You mean date," she accused, trying to inject lightness into her tone.

"Of course, he does," Verna chimed in. "You don't have to take care of us full-time. A little help is appreciated, but don't smother us. Go out with friends. Enjoy life. Don't let work completely rule you."

"Work *does* rule me, Mom." She hugged her mother. "I love what I do, and I love taking care of you. So let me do what makes me happy. I am happy," she repeated, assuring both parents. "And I need to go do some housecleaning and laundry now. Have that shopping list ready for me tomorrow."

She had debts to pay. She knew her parents felt bad that they hadn't been able to finance her education, but Erin felt no resentment over that. A scholarship had covered part of the undergraduate years, and she had taken out loans for the rest. The debts would be repaid in God's timing. He wouldn't have seen her through so much only to abandon her.

She left the house and got into her car. As she reached the city limits of Springfield, her cell phone rang. She checked the caller ID and pressed the device to her ear. "What's on your mind?" she asked her best friend, Ginger Brewer.

"Food," Ginger responded without hesitation. "I've eaten almost nothing all day, and I'm starved. Can you join me at the steak house?"

"I have housework and laundry waiting for me."

"But you have to eat."

She was right. "Okay. I'm about ten minutes from there. See you."

Erin drove to the restaurant and had to wait for Ginger on the parking lot, but it was only about five minutes until she arrived.

Her friend was director of a health and hospice center located in one of the city's strip malls. She and Erin had been friends in elementary school and remained close through high school graduation. Over the next few years they had kept in touch, but hadn't seen much of one another. But after finishing their schooling and returning to the area, their close relationship had resumed as if they had never been apart. And their careers were similar enough to add an additional bond. Living in the same town was another plus.

When they had ordered their meals, Ginger leaned back in her seat and eyed Erin closely. "You look upset. Is your wackadoodle still bugging you?"

Erin winced. "He's become a photography buff and has been spending his breaks walking around the mall, shooting pictures of everything."

"Including you," Ginger added instinctively.

Erin nodded. Freddy James had attended the same high school she and Ginger did, but had not been in their classes. He had an IEP, Individualized Education Program, and attended special education classes in math and reading related subjects. He was good-natured and never in trouble. The problem was that, in high school, he had developed an infatuation with Erin and tried to date her. Not wanting to encourage him, but also not wanting to hurt him, Erin had rejected his date requests as nicely as possible and avoided interaction with him as much as she could. She was civil and polite, but firm in her rejections, yet sometimes found it difficult to manufacture enough excuses to avoid being alone with him.

After being away in college for years and breaking contact with him, Erin thought the cycle had been broken, but a few months after moving into her quarters at the mall, she had unexpectedly encountered Freddy working behind the counter at the fast food shop on the second floor. He had become excited when he recognized her, and his infatuation immediately rekindled.

Ginger frowned. "You need to tell him you've found a sweetheart, or just be blunt and say you don't want to be in a relationship with anyone."

Erin sighed. "I know. You're right. It's just that he's a sweet and harmless guy, and I hate to hurt his feelings. I shouldn't be surprised that he lives here in Springfield, seeing as how so many students move here for jobs or to attend college after high school."

The waitress arrived with their orders, and their attention turned to blessing the food and enjoying their meal. It was late when they parted.

When Erin arrived home, she unlocked and opened the front door of her little house. And heard a muffled sound from inside as she entered. A subtle shift in the atmosphere made the hair on the back of her neck stand on end.

She froze in reaching for the light switch, her heart pounding. Suddenly something powerful slammed into her from the darkness. Pain exploded in her head, and she crumpled to her knees.

An arm reached under her arm and yanked her to her feet. "Where is it?" a voice grated in her ear.

"I don't know what you're talking about," she gasped, ramming her elbow backward into his gut. His grip didn't loosen.

"What did you do with it?" he persisted.

This time she jammed her foot down on his instep. He yelped, and his grip loosened just enough for her to jerk free of his hold. She lunged forward and shot out of the house through the still open doorway.

Help me, Lord. Please.

As footsteps pounded behind her, Erin's purse slipped from her shoulder. She tripped over it and stumbled to the sidewalk. In a reflexive motion, she rolled to her back, raised her right foot, and kicked as hard as she could at her assailant's legs.

He grunted and stumbled forward as her heel connected with the calf of his right leg. His head turned, and fear glazed eyes stared back at her through the ski mask holes.

A flash of recognition hit Erin, and she scrambled to her feet. She snatched the strap of her purse, visualizing the phone in the side pocket of it.

Her attacker jumped to his feet and started toward her, but halted at the sound of an approaching vehicle. He whirled and ran. Within seconds he had rounded the corner of her little house and fled from sight.

Erin dug her phone from her purse and dialed the police as she struggled to her feet.

"Wait right there," she was instructed when she reached someone, identified herself and gave a rapid fire explanation of what had happened. She disconnected, walked the few yards back to her front porch and plopped onto the top step to wait.

Her thoughts whirled. She made a study of eyes, and she was sure she had detected fear in the eyes of that mask covered face. The body had been near the same height and weight of the thief who had collided with her in the parking lot, and he was looking for something.

Concentrating, a vision of the contents of her purse strewing over the lot came to mind. Had the guy dropped something when he fell? If so, could it have fallen among the items strewn from her purse and been scooped up with them?

Erin jerked the purse from her side to her lap and began rummaging inside it. She noticed nothing out of the ordinary, so stopped looking when a police cruiser pulled to the curb in front of the house and an officer emerged from it.

"I'm Officer Grady," the middle-aged officer introduced himself as he approached, his deep-set gaze skimming over her. "Are you hurt?"

She shook her head and stood. "I'm fine, just mystified."

He frowned. "How so?"

"When the guy attacked me, he demanded to know where *it* is, and I have no idea what he was talking about."

The officer frowned. "So this was no random robbery. Someone was after something. Do you know who it was? Anyone you recognized?"

"He wore a ski mask, so I'm not certain, but I think it was the young man who plowed into me in the mall parking lot when he was running from the security guard."

"When was that?" He pulled a notepad and pen from his pocket.

"This afternoon as I was on my way to my car after work."

"You work at the mall?"

She nodded and told him which mall. "My optometry practice is located there."

His expression grew thoughtful. "I think I need to talk to that security guard. You may have identified his thief."

Erin sat quietly while he called his headquarters, obtained a number and called the guard's cell number. "The guard says he's off duty, but he'll be here in ten minutes," he said after he disconnected.

Two minutes sooner than that, a navy-blue pickup pulled to the curb. The man who emerged was dressed in jeans and a tee shirt rather than in uniform, but there was no mistaking the replacement security guard she had met hours earlier.

His dark eyes gleamed in a ruddy face, topped by dark hair that fell over his forehead without making him look boyish. He struck Erin as tough and capable, all lean muscle and lithe movements.

As she pushed to her feet, he extended a hand.

"I don't think we introduced ourselves this afternoon. I'm Miles Jarrett. Officer Grady tells me you think the intruder who attacked you here in your home is my smash and grab guy. I understand that you're Doctor Stuart." His eyes narrowed in scrutiny.

"I am, but please call me Erin. I think it was the same person, but I can't be absolutely certain." She placed her hand in his briefly and withdrew it, taken off guard by the shivers that danced up her arm. If she wasn't mistaken, she saw a similar jolt of surprise on his face.

"Is anything missing?"

"I don't know. I haven't gone back inside and looked around."

"Let's do that now."

The three of them entered the house, and the officers accompanied Erin from room to room while she checked and determined, even though a few items had been disturbed, that nothing seemed to be missing. "I guess I arrived home before he had time to find what he was looking for or take anything else."

"Will you tell me everything that happened, just like you did for Officer Grady?"

Erin went back over her brief story.

"Did you see his face?" he asked when she finished.

She shook her head. "He wore a ski mask, but the build of his body and the way he ran looked just like that guy running away on the parking lot."

"Did you see a car?"

"No. He ran around the side of the house, so he must have been parked somewhere back there and entered the building from the rear. I haven't checked the kitchen door or windows yet."

"Let's do that now."

Erin cringed when the officers found that the back door lock had been jimmied. "He didn't hurt me. Do you think he would have if I hadn't gotten away?"

Officer Jarrett grimaced. "It's hard to say. He's on police radar as a petty thief. I don't think he's a killer, but when a guy is cornered, anything can happen."

"Does that mean you know who he is?"

His mouth tightened. "I've only been on this job three days, but I've looked through some photos we've been given of persons we're told to watch for and monitor closely if we see them because they've been in trouble multiple times. I think one of those photos is of him. If so, he's a young fellow by the name of Harley Davis. His nickname is Bike."

Erin suppressed a snicker and tried to keep her expression neutral, but a twitch at the corners of his mouth caused her to go ahead and grin. For some reason she didn't understand, it made her aware of him in a new and …stimulating sort of way.

"I tend to think he's just a young man who has gotten in with a bad crowd and may be taking orders from someone. Do you have any idea what he was after?"

"I have no idea," she repeated. "I dropped my purse during that collision in the mall parking lot, and some of my belongings spilled out of it, so I wondered if he had also dropped something and I managed to put it in my purse. I looked, but didn't see anything extra in there."

His gaze on her was so intense that it made her uneasy. She shifted her weight from one foot to the other and gazed past him to where the moon was ascending over the distant Ozark hills.

"If you have any further incidents, or think of any details about what happened, will you contact me?" He took a card from his wallet and handed it to her.

She nodded, taking it. "Sure."

When both officers were gone, Erin showered and went to bed early. After a night of restless sleep, she rose, ate a bowl of cereal and settled in front of the television for a cup of coffee before going to work. Still restless, her mind began to play back over the incident with the intruder, trying to think what *it* could possibly be. Her vision swung to her purse on the sofa.

She picked it up and dumped the contents onto the sofa beside her. Then she raked her fingers through the items. Idly, she picked up the tube of Chapstick, thinking she could use some on her dry lips.

She started to open it, but noticed that the tube label indicated it was cherry flavored. She never bought the flavored kind, only the original. She removed the lid—and stared in shock. Instead of Chapstick inside the tube, she was staring at what looked to be a mini flash drive.

She inhaled a deep breath, her mind whirling. She had to call Miles. She found his card and her cell phone and started to dial, but changed her mind. She was headed to work within minutes. She would just leave now and take it to him.

Chapter 2

Miles had only been on duty about an hour Thursday morning when he spotted the eye doctor coming down the wide hallway toward him. She walked with a sense of purpose, and her gaze intensified when it lit on him.

When she came to a halt before him, he breathed in the scent of her freshly laundered blue dress and white lab coat, along with a subtle floral scent.

Why did he find her so attractive? He didn't know. And he couldn't afford to get involved on a personal level with her. He couldn't go down that route with anyone. Never again. He quickly refocused. "What's on your mind?"

"I found something," she said softly, after glancing around as if to be sure no one was near enough to hear.

"Come with me." He escorted her to the security office a few feet away, closed the door and stood near the desk.

When she extracted a tube of Chapstick from her purse, his chest tightened in anticipation. He drew a deep breath when she removed the cap and showed him the inside of it.

"*That's* the *it* he was after. It has to be," she said with surety.

When she offered it to him, he took it. "When did you find this?"

"This morning when I started to use some Chapstick and discovered the tube isn't the kind I use. It's labeled cherry, and I only use the original," she explained with a touch of dryness.

"I'll see that this gets to the proper person." He didn't explain that he was the proper person and would contact his superior as soon as he examined it. "Thanks for bringing it directly here."

"I started to call, but I was already heading to work. I need to get back to my office now. I have an appointment in a few minutes."

He opened the door for her and watched as she walked back toward her office. She had been drawn into this mess by sheer chance, but he suspected it was a good break for him.

He turned on his heel and moved to the desk. As soon as the computer booted, he inserted the flash drive and opened it. What he found was a collection of photos and a couple of documents. The photos were of businesses in the mall, including Erin's, and some shots of the mall surroundings, as well as some of assorted outdoor scenery and vehicles.

He didn't know what to make of them. They seemed innocent enough, but was there a connection that wasn't obvious? There were too many of them, and no apparent relevance. They would require detailed examination to determine if anything was of significance to the drug operators they were after.

Since Erin's shop was part of the mall, and her home had been breached, she needed to be watched closely—and protected.

That decided, Miles moved on from the photos and opened one of the files. Or tried to. It was password protected. With no idea of a possible password, he tried the second file—and had no problem opening it. It contained a list of names, obviously code identities for people, either cutesy or downright dumb.

Wee Duds – M
Old Nag– W
Ringer – F
Worm – S

They didn't make sense to Miles. He called Jed Parker. "I need Julian to take a look at something," he said when his superior answered. Julian was their tech expert. Miles explained what he had and described the contents. "After Julian examines it, can you have him do whatever it takes to get a look at Bike's Facebook page and look for anything interesting in his messages?"

"Send those files to his secure server, and I'll discuss it with him," Jed promised.

Miles's phone sounded an incoming call. "Thanks. I have to take another call."

~

"Do these make a statement?" Lydia Carmichael turned from her computer to face Erin, her face scrunched up in a grin. She reached up and tweaked the arrangement of her nearly white bangs above the frames she wore.

Erin tipped her head, studying her assistant's latest eyewear. Lydia didn't need glasses, but wore the current eyewear trends as a fashion statement, and purportedly as advertisement of their product. These latest ones were tortoiseshell frames in a dusted pink. Erin suspected Lydia had selected them because she thought they made her appear intelligent.

"I think they're becoming." Not overly fond of the horn-rimmed style, Erin held back a smile. Lydia could be a bit over dramatic at times. In her late thirties, she had just decided to change jobs when Erin opened this office. Her experience fit what was needed, and she had worked out well in spite of her absorption with fashion to the point of flashiness.

Lydia's expression morphed into a frown. "Just before you came in, I heard you were attacked in your home last night. Is that true?"

Erin nodded. "It is."

"Was it a robbery?"

"It may have been an attempt at one, but nothing was taken."

"Because you arrived home too soon?"

"It's possible." Erin started to mention the person demanding to know where *it* was, and then finding the flash drive, but didn't, thinking the police surely would want that kept confidential.

Lydia tipped her head, studying her. "Are you okay?"

"I'm fine. Who's our first appointment?"

Lydia faced her computer and glanced at the screen. "It's Ruth Jansen, but it's not for ten minutes yet. Your mother called," she added, swiveling the desk chair back around.

"Did she say what she wanted?"

"No, and I didn't ask. I figured it was private. She just said she'd like to speak to you when you have time."

Erin's parents had likely heard about the home invasion. It was only right that they hear a firsthand account from her. "I'll give her a ring."

She entered her private office and closed the door. "Here's what happened," she said when her mother answered her call. She related the incident, except for finding the flash drive.

"Do the police have any leads?"

"I'm not sure. I'll check with the security guard when I have some free time."

There was a slight pause before her mother spoke again. "Your dad and I were talking, and we think we'd like to attend the political rally Senator Fielder has scheduled at a

Branson theater on Wednesday. Could you come down after work and take us? Everett wants to ask the man a couple of questions."

Erin stifled a sigh. "What time does it start?"

"Six o'clock."

"I'll pick you up at five-thirty." If she could finish early and go straight from work to get them, they should make it to Branson in time for the rally. They didn't ask favors often, and they needed her. Dad no longer felt comfortable driving at night, which it would be by the end of the rally.

"Thanks, Sweetheart. I know you're busy, so I'll let you go now."

~

Concern for Erin's safety ate at Miles as he passed her office during security rounds Friday morning. At the same time, another compartment of his brain buzzed with the puzzle of what was in the locked file on that flash drive. His gut said it had to do with the drugs flowing through this mall.

As he walked toward the flea market, his inclination was to just raid it and end the drug distribution going on under everyone's noses. But doing that now would only shut down this one operation site. They needed facts, evidence that would lead them to the kingpin behind the plague that was creeping in an ever-increasing reach through the area.

He kept a close eye on the vendors throughout the day, but detected nothing that could be identified as a drug transaction. As he turned to patrol more of the mall, he nearly collided with a woman who was walking briskly and looking down to extract her keys from her purse. When she halted, nearly losing her balance, he placed a hand on her shoulder. And their eyes met.

"Excuse me," Erin said, looking up. Then she took a quick breath of recognition. A flush swept over her face that made amusement and warmth creep through him. He quickly withdrew his hand and stepped back.

"I'm sorry," he apologized. "I wasn't watching my steps and didn't see you."

She grinned. "If you can't see me, maybe you need glasses."

He found himself entranced by the glow of that smile. She had again pulled the top section of her dark blond hair back in a ponytail, letting the lower section fall over her shoulders. The casual yellow tunic edged with lace over a simple tan skirt gave her a carefree look. Only he knew she wasn't carefree.

"Maybe I do need glasses," he said with a grin.

Her smile ebbed as she studied his face, her mouth pursing a bit. "Your eyes look fine, but you could be nearsighted."

"Is your appointment schedule full?" As the words left his mouth, he shocked himself at the uncharacteristic impulse.

She tipped her head. "It was, but we had a cancellation a few minutes ago. It was to have been the last one of the day. Can you come in at four-thirty?"

Miles thought rapidly. Why not, he reasoned. He hadn't seen an eye doctor in a long time, and he had been experiencing some eye fatigue and burning. He was sure it was just from normal tiredness and too much reading, but it wouldn't hurt to be certain. "A checkup wouldn't be a bad idea. I'll get someone to cover for me." He would call Keaton, his fellow agent whose shift started at five, and ask him to come in thirty minutes early.

"See you at four-thirty."

As Erin walked away, he wasn't sure why he was reluctant to see her go. Maybe he had been feeling a little lonely lately. She was too attractive for his peace of mind. And getting romantically involved with anyone was a complication he didn't need. He couldn't risk another loss and grief.

He shook off the thoughts and continued his surveillance. He needed to keep his attention on shutting down the drug traffic in this place. Since he had taken on the identity of the mall security guard, he had to maintain the image and perform the duties of the position.

The retail complex wasn't overly crowded with shoppers today. He finished his rounds and returned to a spot that afforded a good overall view of the flea market. Vendors offered a bit of everything. There were electronics, appliances, clothing for all ages, game consoles, cleaning products, sports equipment and more. He detected nothing out of the ordinary—which was frustrating.

When Keaton arrived, Miles wasted no time hoofing it to the optic center. Inside, the back wall of the spacious room was lined with small shelves where rows of eyeglass frames were displayed. He noted a wealth of styles and colors.

A woman with long, fashionably lightened hair looked up when he entered. "Are you our four-thirty appointment?" she asked politely, taking a form from the stack on her desk and attaching it to a clipboard.

"Yes. My name is Miles Jarrett."

She handed him the clipboard. "Please fill out this form. Then the doctor will see you."

He went to a seat and began filling in the requested information. He used the address of the small complex of furnished apartments where he was staying and answered the general health questions honestly, but skipped the ones about insurance, not about to list his employer provided plan. He would just pay cash.

He had just signed the form when Erin appeared in the doorway at the back of the room, a pretty sight. "I'm ready for you now," she said to him before addressing her assistant. "Lydia, I know you have an appointment, so you may go ahead and leave."

Lydia nodded. "I will as soon as I have everything in order."

"Please be seated." Erin pointed at a chair as Miles entered the exam room. When she closed the door, the room seemed suddenly much smaller with only the two of them inside the enclosed space. The air around her seemed electric, charged with a rare voltage.

His chest constricting, Miles sank into the chair—and forced his gaze to the eye chart in front of him. Then he glanced at the framed licenses on another section of the wall. "You must have spent a lot of time in school to become a doctor. Why specialize in eye care?"

Her expression remained pleasant, but purely professional. "Helping my blind mother is how God prepared me to help others."

He frowned. "Has she been blind all her life?"

Erin's face clouded a bit. "No. She was diagnosed with diabetes when she was a girl. It progressed to retinopathy and blinded her when she was in her early fifties. I was in junior high."

"So she became the inspiration behind your career choice." He turned in the seat to face her.

"I suppose that's where it started, but I honestly feel it's a way I can minister to people with vision problems. I learned a lot helping Mom learn to function after she lost her sight, and a passion for others grew from it."

She moved to the nearby wheeled stool, sat and rolled closer to him.

Her saying that God had placed her in the profession took him off guard. In his line of work, he didn't hear too much credit given to God for positive things. "How much schooling did it require?"

She shifted the chair to one side and pointed at the eye chart. "I completed a four-year undergraduate degree and then four more years at a school of optometry—and have the debt to show for it." She smiled, not seeming troubled by the fact.

He focused on the chart.

All business now, she checked his close and distance vision, peripheral vision, and then for his color perception. When that was done, she paused. "Now I need to dilate your eyes with some drops so I can test for glaucoma. Do you have someone to drive you home?"

He shrugged. "I hadn't thought about that, but I can take a taxi."

Seeming satisfied, she proceeded to lean over him and place a drop in each eye. Then she used an instrument that shot a puff of air into his eyes. None of that was pleasant, but it wasn't painful. It was the nearness required to perform the tasks that was unsettling. Especially when he breathed in the scent of something that reminded him of lilacs.

"Everything looks fine," she pronounced when she finished all the tests. "But it's a good idea to have your vision checked regularly."

"How long will the effects of the drops last?" he asked, needing a distraction.

She propelled the stool backward and placed the tool in a drawer. "Typically, anywhere from four to twenty-four hours, but I didn't use the heaviest strength. And darker colored eyes tend to recover faster than lighter colored ones."

"So if you drove us to a nice restaurant we could get to know one another better over a leisurely meal, and I could probably drive myself home afterward." He couldn't believe he had let the crazy notion slip from his mouth.

~

Erin went motionless. Had she heard right? "You want me to take you to supper?"

A flush of embarrassment crossed his face. "Oops. No, I want to take you to supper, but you said I can't drive, so I …"

"It's okay," she interrupted, a bit amused at seeing the disciplined guard thrown off his stride. She glanced over at the wall clock. "My assistant is gone, and my appointments are finished. I can drive us to supper."

He hesitated, his hands on the chair arms in preparation for rising. "I'm sorry. You probably have other plans."

"No, as a matter of fact, I don't. Give me a couple of minutes to put a few things away and get my purse. Then I'll meet you in the waiting room."

"You drive, I pay," he said firmly, opening the exam room door for them to exit.

When they left the front office together minutes later, she noted Miles squinting to view the area around them. "Are you always on alert?" she asked, his uniform reminding her that he had come directly from work duty.

He nodded slightly. "It's second nature, I guess."

"Do you encounter much trouble here in the mall?" she asked as they walked to the exit.

"Our biggest problem is …shoplifting."

Erin had the oddest feeling that he wanted, or started, to say something else. But she refrained from commenting on it. She did, however, notice that he acted more than just alert, as if he sensed something.

Which was odd. Because she did, too. It was as if eyes were penetrating her back. "Do you think we're being watched?" she asked as they walked past the flea market.

"I think it's always possible." He pushed the exit door open, facing her at an angle and squinting. "Are you saying you feel that way?"

She started to deny it, but didn't. "I'm probably being paranoid."

His eyes scanned behind them, blinking. She sensed his frustration. "Let's get out of here. How do you feel about Stan's Steakhouse?"

Some of the tension left his face. "Their buffet is great."

"Do you eat there often?" she asked as they headed toward her white Camaro. She pulled keys from her purse and clicked the button to unlock it.

"I've been there a couple of times since finding it."

"Are you not from here?" She looked across the seat at him once they were inside the car.

"I grew up in Cape Girardeau, but I haven't lived there since high school."

"I know a lot of law enforcement people have military backgrounds. Is that the case with you?"

He nodded. "I served four years in the army. And, yes, I was an MP."

She grinned at his having anticipated her next question.

When they arrived at the steakhouse, there was a line of customers at the door, but it moved quickly. They filled their plates from the salad bar and found a table. Their steaks were delivered before they finished their salads.

Involuntarily her gaze went to his left hand. "I assume since you don't wear a ring that you're not married."

"I'm not."

The naked emotion that glazed his eyes stunned her. "What did I say wrong?"

He shook his head. "You said nothing wrong. And I understand your concern that you might be consorting with a married man. Innocently, of course. I was married years ago."

Erin wasn't sure how to respond. Her hand clenched around her tea glass.

"She died," he continued, calm now. Controlled. "She had a heart condition. We were very young and only married two years."

"I'm sorry." The words seemed so inadequate.

"I guess I should ask if you're married."

She released a wry laugh. "Yes. To my job," she added quickly when his head made a startled jerk.

He leaned forward, his gaze intent. "Aren't you interested in marriage?"

"I have no time for it." She hated what she had seen happen to so many marriages. And, although she might speak lightly of her debt, she did have to practice financial diligence and bore some strain from the weight of those seemingly endless college loan payments.

He frowned. "I guess I understand that. My job also takes most of my time. I draw a lot of overtime," he added, as if clarifying, or justifying, the claim.

They focused on their meal, the personal subject dropped, but Erin couldn't help being aware of the electricity vibrating between them. She wondered if he felt it as well. And reprimanded herself for even thinking such a thing. Neither of them had the time or interest for relationships.

"How much has your vision cleared?" She gazed at his dark orbs.

He put his fork down and raised his face. "Actually, I think it's about back to normal. I should be able to drive by the time we get back to the mall."

"That's rushing a bit."

He considered for a moment, and then grinned. "I'm seeing fine, but how about I drive carefully and you follow me to my apartment to make sure I arrive okay? We'll add your cell phone number to my contacts. You already have my card, so you can call me if you think I'm driving dangerously."

"All right," she agreed, hoping she wasn't making a mistake.

They finished their dessert, and she drove him back to his truck at the mall. Then they caravanned to an apartment complex where Miles parked in front of number 128. She gave him a friendly wave and headed home.

Erin stiffened when she pulled into her driveway and saw that her front door was open. She parked at the garage entrance and approached the house. When she peered inside, she gasped.

~

Miles had just entered his apartment and turned on the television when his cell phone rang. Alarm shot through him when he saw it was Erin. "What's wrong?"

"My house has been ransacked." Her voice was a tad strident, but controlled.

"I'll be right there. Wait out front for me."

Five minutes later, he found her standing next to her car in the driveway, her expression thunderous. He couldn't blame her for being upset.

She followed him up the steps, where he found that the door lock had been smashed. He pulled out his weapon and moved cautiously inside, knowing she was right behind him.

She gasped at the sight of strewn papers and an overturned lamp table. The bedroom was also a mess, the dresser drawers pulled open and clothes torn from their hangers.

"Someone is searching for something," she whispered from near his shoulder. "Do you think it's that flash drive?"

"That's exactly what I think." Miles gripped her elbow and steered her back to the living room.

"What's so important about it?" she asked in a strained voice. "Don't they realize I found it and gave it to you?"

"Apparently not." He weighed the situation rapidly. He had to give her some explanation. "I have to call the police so they can take print samples and look for evidence. But there's something I need to tell you. Let's go to the porch, and I'll explain while we wait for them."

He doubted they would find anything incriminating, though. Bike had been around the block with the justice system and would have known to wear gloves.

He guided her back out onto the porch and to the top step while dialing the police. He sat, tugging her down beside him. After completing the call, he met her gaze. "I'm not a mall security guard."

Chapter 3

Erin's gaze locked on him, not quite comprehending. "Then what are you?"

He reached back and pulled an ID wallet from his pocket and showed it to her. "I'm Miles Jarrett, like I told you, but I'm a DEA agent posing as a security guard."

She peered at the credentials. "So what are you doing at the mall?"

He rubbed a hand over his jaw. "Considering the way you've been drawn into it, I believe you deserve some explanation and will keep the information confidential. We think drugs are being funneled through the flea market. They're hidden in products handled by some of the vendors and sold right under everyone's noses."

"And you're working undercover to catch them," she blurted, the picture coming together rapidly. "That's why you asked so many questions."

"Yes."

She frowned. "If you know that, why aren't you arresting people?"

A grim expression crossed his face. "We need more information. Evidence. And we don't know who the power is behind the operation—and possibly other schemes. Your office is located near there. Have you noticed any suspicious activities?"

Erin's head rotated back and forth. "I had no idea."

"If we don't stop the flow of drugs in the area, crime will continue to rise, as will drug-related deaths."

Her mouth went dry as she grasped the realities. "You want to catch the mastermind, not just the low-level minions."

"That's right. And I suspect you've accidentally landed in the mess. I think the thug who plowed into you is more than just a thief. I don't know his connection, though."

"Do you know what's on that flash drive I gave you?"

"Photographs and a couple of files. But one of the files is password protected, and the other is a list that doesn't make sense."

She frowned. "You mean it's coded?"

He grimaced. "It's nothing sophisticated, but we haven't figured it out yet. Our tech expert is working on it."

More reality penetrated her brain. "The guy who dropped it thinks I still have that drive."

"I'm afraid so. Which is both good and bad. It means he doesn't know you've given it to me, which is good. But he's still after it, and that's bad. Will you take extra precautions?"

The seriousness of the matter frightened her, but she couldn't crawl in a hole and hide. "I'll be careful," she promised. "But I have to work—and live my life."

"I'll keep an eye on your place and alert you if I see Bike in the mall."

As he spoke, his phone rang. He answered and spoke briefly. "I'm on my way." He stood and headed down the steps. "Be careful," he said as he hurried away.

Taking his warning to heart, Erin locked her house and spent the weekend in Ozark with her parents. It was such a normal practice that she kept a supply of clothing there, so they suspected nothing out of the ordinary. This weekend she took them to visit Mom's sister Saturday afternoon, and then to Sunday morning services at the church they had joined after Dad's retirement.

Everett had felt that they should not stay at the church where he had spent the last eight years of his ministry, not wanting to risk having his presence intrude on a new pastor's leadership in any way. Loyal members had a tendency to follow old habits and seek advice from the pastor they had already come to know and trust, unwittingly undermining the new pastor's confidence.

Sunday evening Erin returned to her house in Springfield and found no evidence of disturbance, which made her feel a bit better. When she received a text from Miles—one of several over the weekend— asking how she was doing, she took pleasure in informing him of that fact. But she followed his instructions and made sure all doors and windows were securely locked before going to bed.

Once she reached the mall entrance Monday morning, Erin again experienced the eerie sensation of being watched. She scanned the area, but saw nothing out of the ordinary. She continued to her office, greeted Lydia on entry, and went about an ordinary day. In addition to primary eye care examinations, she provided contact lens fittings, management and treatment of ocular disease, and LASIK consultation. Her Monday through Friday appointment calendar stayed full most of the time.

During a brief mid-morning break between appointments, she called in a lunch order to the food mart on the second floor, planning to stay inside the office and eat at her desk that day. But during the next exam she discovered she was out of ink in her printer, and there was none in the supply cabinet.

Needing to print a report, she grabbed her purse and went to the front office where Lydia was speaking on the phone, making an appointment. "You're busy," Erin said softly. "I'm going to run to the office supply store. Be right back."

Lydia nodded and continued her conversation.

Erin was walking down the hallway, intent on her errand, when she was bumped from behind. Then a hand grabbed her purse and yanked. Hard.

She gasped and clutched the strap that circled her shoulder, hanging on for dear life. As her assailant gave another sharp yank, she instinctively whirled and screamed. Then, her heart thudding, she abruptly dropped to the floor, swung her legs around and kicked as hard as she could.

As the guy stumbled forward and landed on all fours, she heard him groan and utter a curse. Before he could get to his feet, she kicked him again.

As people shouted and hovered nearby, the guy staggered to his feet, stumbled and fled.

"What happened?"

Erin looked up to find Miles coming to a sliding halt next to her. She pointed. "Someone tried to snatch my purse. He's getting away."

Miles took off in pursuit. But he returned a couple of minutes later, meeting her in the hall where she had followed him after making it to her feet. "He had too much of a head start and disappeared in the parking lot. Are you okay?"

She nodded, clutching her purse in her right hand while rubbing the aching left one. "My shoulder was wrenched, but I'm fine."

He studied her. "You shouldn't be out here alone. Where were you going?"

"The office supply store for printer ink."

"I'll escort you."

He did and waited while she made her purchase. "Do you think your attacker was Bike?" he asked as they walked back to her office.

She shook her head. "No. This guy was shorter and skinnier."

He paused at the door of her unit. "I want you to promise me you'll not leave your office alone again. I'll escort you to your car after work and follow you home. I want you to pack an overnight bag and spend the night somewhere else."

Erin hated to do that, but she understood. "I spend a lot of nights with my parents, but I don't want to frighten them or put them at risk."

"I'll explain the situation to them, and we can see how it affects them. Do they live nearby?"

"They're in Ozark."

"The guy who attacked you was sent to get that drive and probably doesn't know you personally, so you should be safe there," he decided after a few moments of consideration. "I'll meet you right here when you're ready to go. Do you always leave work at five?"

"Yes."

"I'll be here."

Lydia looked up when Erin entered the office. "Your next appointment is already in an exam room. I heard a racket from up the hallway. What happened?"

Erin didn't want to explain, but she did.

Lydia's eyes widened behind the oversized square eyeglass frames of the seventies and eighties that she wore today. "That's awful. I wish they had caught the guy."

Erin nodded and hurried to her private office. She dumped the ink cartridges on her desk, pulled a lab coat over her light gray blouse that she had paired with black slacks, and then hurried to meet her patient.

She had just stepped into the waiting room after completing the exam when the door opened, and a man wearing a shirt and hat bearing the name of the food mart pushed a delivery cart inside. It was Freddy, exactly what she did not need right now.

"Hey," he practically yelled at her appearance, letting the door swing shut behind him. "What happened a while ago? I heard somebody tried to hurt you." Concern rang in his voice, his eyes round beneath a fringe of dark brown hair and thick brows.

"I don't think he meant to hurt me," she corrected. "He just tried to take my purse."

Freddy's brow furrowed. "You mean he just wanted money?"

"That's what I'd guess." She wasn't about to mention those other incidents to anyone besides Miles or the police. "Is that my lunch you have there?"

"Oh, yeah." He picked up one of the containers and handed it to her.

"Wait just a jiffy and I'll pay you." Erin dashed to her office and pulled her wallet from her purse, thankful she still had it.

Freddy had just taken her money when Erin heard her phone ringing inside her office. "Thanks, Freddy. I have to get that." She hurried back to her desk, thankful for the reprieve.

The caller was Miles. "Can you look at surveillance footage with me right after work?"

"Sure," she said, setting her food on the desk.

~

As he strolled through the mall, making his presence known, Miles speculated about which of the flea market vendors were dealing drugs. After studying them all week, he had to admit the sellers were slick, whoever they were. The goods were well concealed and smoothly handled. He pulled out his phone, opened the surveillance app and scrolled through images, viewing locations outside the building and then the businesses inside. All looked clear. Good.

Moving on, his gaze sharpened on the flea market booths. He wondered where Leland Zink, the owner, was. He didn't see how the man's business could be at the center of a drug ring and him not be aware of it—most likely at the head of it. But he hadn't been able to spot the man in anything incriminating.

The guy didn't seem to have a regular schedule. Miles had only met him a few times. Leland hadn't been overly friendly, but neither had he been unfriendly when Miles had encountered him during rounds. The man had given him an impression of someone absorbed in his business—and little else.

Miles had checked into whether Leland had an office of any kind on the premises and found no evidence of one. He could be working out of his home, or anywhere, for that matter.

Drawn from his musings, Miles focused on a figure that had just emerged from a sport shop. The thirtyish, tousle headed man carried a camera and was taking pictures of the area. His camera didn't look very sophisticated. He focused on the optometry shop and snapped a shot.

Ignoring the sounds of human traffic, chatter and occasional laughter inside the retail complex, Miles approached the amateur photographer.

The fellow came to an abrupt halt, his eyes wide. "What's wrong, Officer?"

"I just wondered about your picture taking. Is there a reason for it, or is it just for fun?"

A grin crossed the man's boyish face. "I work here now, and I have friends here. And I like to take pictures."

Miles glanced across the hall. "Is the doctor one of your friends?"

The guy's face lit. "Oh, yeah. She was my friend way back in high school. And now she's my friend again."

Suddenly Miles thought he recalled seeing this guy in a uniform and pushing a cart. "What's your name?"

"I'm Freddy James," he said, his chest expanding in pride.

"Where do you work?"

"At one of the food marts upstairs. I really like the job. I just got it this summer."

He seemed harmless. "It's good to hear you say you like your job. I guess I'll be seeing you around."

Head bobbing, Freddy hurried away.

Noting the time, Miles headed to the optometry office to meet Erin. He took up a position a few feet from the door.

"Are you ready to watch some footage?" he asked when she emerged, her purse hanging from its shoulder strap but clutched closely to her side.

She locked the door. "Show me what you have."

They walked directly to the little security office where the footage was visible on the flat screen where he had paused it. He dragged another chair next to the one already there. Once they were seated side by side, he started the feed playing.

"The angles are good, but the guy moving up behind you keeps his head low, never looking up. And the baseball hat he's wearing hides his face."

When Erin scooted forward in her chair, he played the segment again. She studied it intently, but then shook her head and shifted back in the chair. "It's a good view of him grabbing my purse, but I can't see his face at all." Frustration laced her voice.

"And you're sure he's not familiar to you?"

"No. All I'm sure of is that it's not Bike. The body build is too different."

"Well, thanks for trying." He turned in the chair to face her. "I need to catch this guy, and I need to find out what's in that flash drive file. The drug operation has to be stopped. The problems are accelerating."

She gave him a sympathetic look that was tinged with curiosity.

He weighed how much to reveal, but decided that she needed to understand the scope of the problem. "That call I took just before leaving your place Friday evening was from the local police captain. They found a young mother dead of an overdose in her car, her baby in a carrier seat beside her."

Horror spread over Erin's countenance. "Where?"

"The car was at the back edge of the mall parking lot. Fortunately, a window was open. Someone heard the baby crying and then noticed the mother slumped in the seat. The woman called the police, and officers arrived in time to keep the baby from suffocating in the heat."

Erin's face had gone pale. "You think she bought the drugs from someone in the mall and immediately took some."

"I'm afraid so." He couldn't keep the bad feeling in the pit of his stomach from punctuating his tone. He had to change the subject. "I met a fellow who says he's a friend of yours."

Her expression turned a bit wary. "Oh?"

"He was taking pictures, including of your business. So I spoke to him."

Her eyes rolled upward. "Did he say his name is Freddy?"

"He did."

She drew a deep breath. "He had a crush on me in high school."

He sensed it had been deeper than a simple crush. "Infatuation?"

She nodded. "I tried to keep from hurting his feelings, but I couldn't encourage him. For years after graduation I hadn't seen him, and then one day a few weeks ago I encountered him at a food mart."

"And the infatuation revived," he concluded intuitively.

She nodded. "He's a good guy, was never in trouble. But he …well, he wasn't very …academic."

"I get the picture," he assured her. "Has he become a problem?"

"No, but I do my best to keep things impersonal when I encounter him."

"Are you ready for me to follow you home? I'm off duty now."

"Yes."

As she drove off the parking lot, Miles stayed close behind her, sensing that she needed protection. They were also on alert regarding her friend Freddy. The guy seemed harmless, yet he couldn't help but recall the photos on that flash drive and make an association to Freddy's camera.

Chapter 4

When Erin pulled into the driveway of her parents' frame house, she could see in her rearview mirror that Miles was right behind her, having insisted on escorting her to Ozark and meeting her parents. He joined her at the door of her car as she stepped out of it.

The front door of the house swung open as they walked up the steps onto the porch where her mother stood in the opening. Verna wore comfy slacks and a lightweight blouse, but didn't carry her cane, not needing it in the familiarity of her own home.

Erin placed a hand on her companion's arm. "Mom, I'd like you to officially meet Miles Jarrett. Miles, this is my mother, Verna Stuart."

He shook the hand extended to him. "It's good to meet you, Mrs. Stuart. I can see the resemblance between you and your daughter."

"Thank you." Verna smiled and stepped back, motioning for them to enter.

As Miles stepped just inside the room, Erin wondered what he thought of her parents' modest home. It was comfy and welcoming, furnished with an inexpensive gray couch and love seat, a coffee table and two matching end tables. A fireplace took up most of one wall, a family photograph of them and Erin on the mantle.

She saw Miles glance at the photo. But then the smile he directed at her put her at ease.

"Miles is the security guard at the mall, Mother."

Verna frowned. "Have you had more trouble?"

"Someone tried to take her purse," Miles supplied for her. "I hope you can persuade her to stay with you every night for a while."

"We'll do our best," her dad said, rising from the sofa to greet Miles with a handshake. "Does the fact that you're keeping tabs on her mean you'll be attending the political rally she's taking us to Wednesday?"

Miles darted a glance at Erin. "If she's going to be there, I will, too."

"Do you have time for some refreshments?" Mom asked.

Miles shook his head. "It sounds tempting, but I need to get back to the mall. There's some work I need to do in the office. I just wanted to be sure your daughter is settled before leaving."

His shift was over at the mall, so Erin assumed he had DEA work in mind. Keeping up the security guard image while also working his agency's case had to be demanding.

Mom's head tilted. "You have an interesting voice. This is one of the times I wish I could see someone."

If Erin wasn't mistaken, she detected a note of speculation in her mother's gentle voice.

Miles darted a quizzical look at Erin.

She shrugged. "Mom may be blind, but she has sharp instincts."

"You handle yourself so well I would never have guessed if Erin hadn't mentioned it."

Mom smiled. "I can no longer physically see my worldly surroundings, but I know they're here. It's like that with our creator. He can't be seen with the physical eye, but I know with certainty He exists."

"She can't do a lot of things," Dad interjected, moving to stand beside her. "There are also many things she can do, but Erin and I do all the driving and take her shopping. Erin helps in many other ways," he added, affection so clear in the words that a flush of embarrassment crept up her neck.

"Thank you for looking after Erin," her mother said.

"Glad to do it," he responded with a smile before leaving.

~

Back at the mall, summer daylight still prevailed. Miles soon found his partner on duty.

"What are you doing back here?" Keaton's eyes scanned the area as he spoke.

He knew about everything up until today, but needed to be brought up to date on the purse snatching attempt, Freddy, and where Erin was staying.

"I want to look at those flash drive files again and do some research on a couple of guys. When I'm done, I'll fill you in on anything I find, plus today's happenings. You go ahead and make your presence felt out here."

Miles entered the office and turned on the computer. While it booted, he called Julian. "Have you had any luck with that flash drive?"

"Yeah, I was just about to call you. But you won't be happy with what I found," the savvy tech expert said.

"Let me have it."

"I got into that password-protected file. It's just a letter."

"Read it to me."

"Hold on a second while I pull it onto my screen." There was a pause. "Okay, here it is."

Miles listened closely as Julian read.

I have facts and names and proof. If you don't want the police to know everything, you'll give me $20,000. If it's not in the place I said by the time I said, you bite the dust.

"So it's about blackmail," Miles muttered when Julian finished. "It's a letter Bike sent to someone. But it doesn't list any names and information."

"I warned you that you'd be disappointed," Julian reminded him.

"Shoot me a copy of that note. Thanks," he added before ending the call.

Foremost in his mind was that he had to find Bike. The guy apparently wasn't very smart if he thought he could blackmail whoever was behind an operation of this magnitude.

Miles went to a search engine and entered the name Harley Davis. When a list of hits appeared on the screen, he clicked on the first one. The article was about an arrest for breaking and entering.

It took some more searching before he came up with an address. As soon as he did, Miles located Keaton and gave him the promised updates. Then he went to his pickup.

After leaving the mall parking lot, he drove to a low-income apartment complex and parked near the unit listed as Bike's address. He went to the door and knocked. No one answered.

As he returned to his truck, two young men came strolling around the side of the building to the parking lot. They wore baggy shorts and rumpled tee shirts. Both had dirty brown mops of hair that needed trimming. They darted glances at him and veered away.

"Do you guys know Harley Davis?" Miles called to them. "His nickname is Bike."

One shook his head. "Nope."

The other one frowned, eyeing the uniform Miles still wore. "I think he's one of the guys who hangs around down at the park." He pointed down the street.

Miles headed that way. And found two young men leaning against the side of an older car at the curb, talking to a young woman. All three watched his approach with wary expressions.

The young, ebony haired gal produced a near sneer when asked if they knew Bike. "Don't know the guy."

"And if we did, we wouldn't tell you," one of the guys said bluntly, his tone conveying that they wouldn't tell a cop.

The other guy just smirked.

"Well, if you see him, tell him to stop by the mall so we can chat."

"We'll tell him," the gal said, her tone oozing sarcasm.

Chalking up the outing as a run down a rabbit hole, Miles headed to his apartment. But he couldn't help but think that one of those guys resembled Erin's would-be purse snatcher in height, weight and bulk.

~

The political rally, held in one of the numerous Branson theaters the politicians had somehow secured for the afternoon, wasn't as boring as Erin had anticipated. Her dad managed to ask his two questions about the effect of some legislation on their local economy, and the crowd in attendance seemed genuinely engaged in what the senator had to say—until near the end when a couple of jokers began shouting out wisecracks and criticism designed to disrupt.

As the senator and his associates left the stage, the hecklers became louder rather than quieter. Erin stood on tiptoe to view them better. The body build and height of one of them reminded her of the guy who had tried to snatch her purse. She patted Mom's hand. "I'll be right back."

As she edged her way amongst the milling crowd, Erin observed two things almost simultaneously. Miles, having managed to become part of the security on duty, approached the hecklers from one direction. And one of the hecklers— the one who reminded her of her purse snatcher—looked over and made eye contact with her. His eyes rounded in what looked like recognition.

Miles grabbed the companion's arms and pointed toward the exit, clearly telling them they had to leave. The guy staring at Erin jerked his head around. And then she saw a look of sheer terror cross his face.

As Erin followed the guy's line of vision, she spotted movement in the balcony of the theater. Then suddenly there was a loud crack of gunfire. And the familiar looking heckler crumpled to the floor.

As screams and pandemonium erupted throughout the building, Erin darted a glance back at the figure in the balcony as he whirled and headed out of sight. Instinct kicking in, she sprang into motion, running for the exit and pushing her way through the crush of the crowd. She shoved the door open and raced outside. Pausing for a second, she looked around. Movement to the left caught her eye.

A figure ran across the parking lot from behind the building. When he stopped at a black car and opened the door, he looked her way. His eyes were covered by huge dark glasses, and a long scarf had been looped around his lower face. But she caught a glimpse of pale skin when the scarf slipped.

Time stood still for two long seconds. Then the man ducked into the car. The engine roared to life, tires squealed, and the vehicle sped toward the exit. As it made a right onto the highway, sirens sounded in the distance.

Erin met the first police cruiser that came to a screeching stop a few feet from her. She pointed. "I saw someone leave the balcony and come from the back of the building. He got into a black car and sped off that way."

The officer glanced in the direction she pointed. "Did you get a license number?"

"No," she said, frowning. Her blood froze as a thought flashed through her mind. The shooter didn't know that. He would know there was a chance she had and could identify him.

The officer exited his car, clearly seeing no point in chasing an unidentified car that had already disappeared from view. He raced inside, followed by more officers.

Erin returned inside to find her parents standing next to Senator Fielder.

Dad looked up at her approach. "It looks like the young man is dead. Why would such a thing happen?" Bewilderment etched his expression and voice.

The senator placed a hand on Everett's shoulder. "I don't know, but I'm sure the police will figure it out. My guess is the kid was involved in some kind of feud." He extended a handshake to Erin. "I saw you run out of here. Did you see anything helpful?"

"I saw a car race out of the parking lot." She didn't think she should say any more than that, except to the police if they should ask. Miles would ask, though. She was certain of that.

"It's nice to have met you," the politician said to them collectively. "But I need to talk to the police chief I just saw enter."

They weren't allowed to leave the theater until late evening. Exhaustion swamped Erin, so she knew her parents had to be near the point of collapse. After the hearse had left with the victim, detectives had worked the scene and interviewed witnesses, comparing stories and gathering any shred of evidence they could find.

Miles approached Erin. "You can go now. Take your parents home and stay with them."

She didn't argue, having shared with him about seeing the killer and his car—but not the license plate. "Will you go home, too?"

"No. I'm going to watch video of the parking lot with some other guys and see if we can spot anything."

She nodded. "I'll check in with you tomorrow when I get to work."

~

After the area had been cleared, including the media, Miles joined the police crew to watch theater security footage of the rally.

"Before we get started, let me tell you about that victim," the detective said before the footage started. "His name is Dexter Thornton. He has a record of petty theft, so it's very likely that he's the person who tried to grab the doctor's purse. He's known to hang around the mall with his pals, including Bike and others who have similar records. We think several are involved in petty rackets, but they're all underlings rather than ringleaders."

"I saw the guy at the park late yesterday when I was looking for Bike. Since they're friends, do you think he was after Erin's purse in hopes of finding that flash drive?" Miles asked.

The detective nodded. "I think that's possible. I'll let you know if we find any connection to your drug case," he added before turning his attention to the footage. The action on the flat screen before them, unfortunately, wasn't very helpful.

The theater's regular security guard operated the equipment, and he had stopped it when they spotted the man on the parking lot that fit the description Erin had given them. The huge dark glasses and the scarf draped around the guy's lower face hid his features, as Erin had described.

"Can you zoom in and enlarge the hair?" Miles asked. "Is that a wig he's wearing?"

Everyone leaned forward and studied the image. "I'm sure it is," one of the officers said. Everyone else agreed.

"Will you make a shot of that for me?" Miles asked. "I'd like it for reference."

The theater guard nodded and did as requested.

Miles thanked him and faced Detective Warner once the guard was gone, pleased that Branson law enforcement embraced working in cooperation with him. "I guess that's the best we can do here. What's your overall take on this?"

The veteran detective ran a hand through his salt and pepper hair. "I'm not locked into a theory. You think the victim could be the guy who tried to snatch a purse at the mall, but you can't be certain. One of the Springfield detectives told me they another investigation underway at the mall. Is there any way the porn video operation could be connected?"

His brain whirling, Miles took a long moment to respond. *How could they be related to what had happened here today?*

He shook his head. "I don't know if there's only one boss running rackets, or if either of them extend down here. Either way, I suspect this victim's boss considered him a liability. And if the eye doctor saw the killer, he won't want to risk having her identify him. She's in danger," he added, speaking to himself as much as to the detective. "She's with her parents, and I doubt the guy can locate her with them, but their home needs watching. They live in Ozark."

"If you'll give me that address, I'll call the Ozark department and ask for an officer to be put on surveillance there immediately."

As soon as Miles quoted it, Warner made the call and requested that Dr. Stuart be guarded through the night and followed to work in Springfield the next morning.

When he disconnected, Miles stood. "I'll be waiting at the mall entrance when the doctor arrives, and I'll escort her home after work. We need to keep a car posted by her house any time she's there. And she should be escorted to and from work daily until we know she's safe." He had debated that, after tonight, the closer proximity of staying in her own home in Springfield would make it easier to guard her, but discarded it, not wanting her to be alone.

While driving to his apartment minutes later, his thoughts alternated between the fact that the mall seemed to be a hot bed of criminal activities—and concern about Erin's safety.

As he arrived home, another vision popped into his mind—Freddy and his camera. Could the seemingly innocent guy be caught up in the porn business? Or maybe the drug dealing one as well? The idea seemed preposterous, but appearances and impressions could be deceiving.

And guys like Freddy could be manipulated and used by others.

Chapter 5

Erin didn't sleep well. Visions of the man in that parking lot after the shooting, staring at her from behind those dark glasses, kept replaying in her head. When she crawled out of bed Friday morning and prepared to go to work, she looked out at the police cruiser parked outside her parents' house. She assumed it was not the same one that had followed her home and parked out there, since it was several feet from where that one had been.

When she pulled out of the driveway, it followed her all the way to the employee section of the mall parking lot, but drove away as Miles came from the mall entrance to meet her.

"Good morning," he greeted her, his gaze raking over her rigid posture.

She brushed at her skirt, avoiding eye contact. When his arm slipped behind her waist, her inner muscles fluttered at the contact. She inhaled deeply of the summer air that was already reaching the point of stifling.

"Let's get you inside." He steered her beside him to the mall entrance. "The detective said they've identified that shooting victim as Dexter Thornton, a known associate of Bike, and that they have other friends in common. No one has any idea why he and the guy who was with him and got away were down there at a political rally, other than to make trouble."

Her head whipped around to face him. "You think the guy who was killed was my purse snatcher? Do you think he was looking for that flash drive?"

His expression was grim. "That's our guess on both counts. Whoever he was working for may have decided he failed the job and had him silenced to be sure he didn't shoot off his mouth."

Erin shuddered. "How can anyone be that cold?"

"It's hard to understand."

Suddenly she remembered what she had planned to ask him. "Will you let me look at what's on that flash drive?"

He didn't slow the pace. "I think I can do that. Do you have time right now?"

"I can take time."

"Our tech specialist got the password-protected file open. It's a blackmail letter that indicates the writer knows names and has proof of who is running an operation, which we assume to be the drugs, and he wants twenty thousand dollars to keep quiet. You can view the other file and photos as well."

They entered the mall and went directly to the security office where the computer was already booted. It only took moments for Miles to open a folder. "I sent Julian a copy of the disk," he explained as he unlocked a drawer and took the original from it.

Within moments he had a collage of photos on the screen. "Do you recognize anything in these pictures?"

Erin enlarged and examined them one by one. "They seem like the kind of pictures a tourist would take, just random landscapes, buildings and objects. Some of them are familiar, but I don't see any significance to blackmail."

"Open this text file." He pointed at the one he meant.

She leaned closer, studying the list of odd names and letters that appeared. Then she took a notepad and pen from her purse. "I want to be able to look at this more later. It doesn't mean anything to me now, but maybe I'll get an idea if I keep studying it."

Standing beside her as she wrote, Miles was close enough to touch. When she finished, she looked up—and was gripped by an urge to reach up and feel the rasp of his whiskers against her palm, feel the silkiness of his dark hair. The unexpected impulse shook her.

His eyes darkened, telegraphing that he also felt the …whatever it was between them. Knowing it wasn't one sided was exciting—and scary.

Erin closed her eyes, breaking the connection, and hurriedly pushed to her feet. She stuffed the notepad and pen back into her purse. "Lydia's probably wondering where I am."

He stepped out of the office with her, his hand behind her waist. And they came face to face with Freddy. He glared at their closeness, his camera dangling from a strap clutched in his right hand. Then his chin lifted, his face diffused with anger. "What are you doing with him?" he asked Erin, putting a heavy emphasis on *him*.

Erin suppressed a groan. She didn't need this. "Freddy, I don't owe you any explanation."

Instead of leaving as she had hoped, Freddy turned his attention onto Miles. "You better not be bothering my friend."

"She's my friend, too," Miles said calmly.

"She was my friend first," Freddy shot back, one hand clutching the camera strap and jerking it around in agitation, his normally placid face flushed.

"But you're not my only friend," Erin stated as firmly as she could. "Don't you need to be at work?"

Freddy frowned, staring at her as if she had just betrayed him. Then his hand swung in an arc, and the camera flew toward her.

In a reflexive action, Miles reached out and snagged the flying device. The crack when it hit his palm made Erin wince.

"I think I'd better take this," he told Freddy. "You're handling it dangerously and might hurt someone."

"No!" Freddy jerked the camera to his chest. "You can't have it. It's mine."

"Yes, it is. But you're using it as a weapon. I'll take it, and you can have it back before you go home—if you think you can act responsibly with it." He stressed the *if*. "If you can't, you won't be allowed to have it here in the mall."

Freddy gulped, his eyes wide as he understood that he was in trouble. Then he slowly released the camera strap.

"What time do you get off work?" Miles asked him.

Freddy's throat worked convulsively. "At two. After the lunch rush." His voice was subdued now.

"Okay, run along. And I'll expect you at the security office at five after two to reclaim it."

Erin felt sorry for Freddy, but she couldn't fault Miles for taking his possession.

Once he had the camera, Miles extended his free hand to Freddy. "I'd like to be your friend if you're willing."

When Freddy's gaze darted to Erin, she gave him an arched brow look and an ever so slight nod meant to encourage the move. He glanced briefly at his camera, and then his hand shot out. After a handshake that was even briefer than the glance, he whirled and stalked away.

~

After escorting Erin to her office, Miles watched customers move about the flea market, alert for any suspicious looking activity. One arrest was made for attempted theft, but no drug sales were detected.

Mid-morning, he stopped by the security office and looked at the photos on Freddy's camera. They seemed innocent enough, but he considered the possibility that Freddy could be mapping the mall for someone. It seemed unlikely, but the possibility couldn't be ignored. When Freddy came to get the camera after his work shift, Miles told him to erase all shots taken inside the mall. The fellow wasn't happy about it, but he complied.

Miles had done some online research on Freddy and found no records of criminal charges or even minor trouble in his background. But, as he neared the food marts during afternoon rounds, he entered the one where Freddy worked and asked to speak to the manager.

A thirtyish, apron clad man soon approached the end of the counter. "How may I help you, Officer?"

"I'd like to ask you about an employee."

The manager's expression turned solemn. "Let's go somewhere more private."

Miles followed him into a small office alcove where the man stopped near a desk and faced him. "Which employee are you concerned about?"

"Freddy James."

The name didn't seem to strike a negative response. "He's only been with us a few months, but he seems to like his job, especially delivering call-in orders from shop owners and staff."

"Does he have a good work history?"

The manager frowned. "I only checked with his most recent. He had worked at McDonald's since high school, and he left of his own accord. He told me he had moved to a different apartment, and this is closer to it. I don't know what more I can tell you."

"What about his friends? Does he have any who come around often?"

The man's brow crinkled in concentration. "I do remember seeing a couple of guys talking to him more than once. Freddy stopped by their table while they were eating. I don't know who they are, though. Are you afraid he's keeping bad company?"

"I don't know. I just know he takes a lot of pictures when he's circulating through the mall, and I want to be sure his photography is only a harmless hobby."

The manager's expression lightened. "I'm sure it is."

Miles thanked the man for his time and left.

As he strolled back within sight of the flea market, he shook off the depressing thought of how little progress was being made on anything. Then his brain space was immediately taken over by thoughts of Erin. An emotional attachment seemed to be developing for her, whether he welcomed it or not. The rational part of his mind warned him to steer clear of her, but he couldn't. She was in danger. And he bore responsibility for that.

He wasn't sure what to do about it. He didn't consider himself emotionally strong enough to risk another plunge into a relationship—and loss. The one thing he knew for sure, though, was that he couldn't let personal feelings interfere with his job. His job had become his life. He was good at it and didn't need the distraction of a beautiful woman.

He caught sight of a familiar face at one of the vendor booths and slowed his pace. Then he realized it was Erin's assistant. She looked different in the dapper semi-rimless eyeglass frames she wore today.

She was holding up an item and speaking to Leland, the market owner. "Are you a shopping addict?" Miles asked in a friendly fashion as he approached them.

Lydia whipped her head around and smiled when she recognized him. "I confess. I am. What do you think of this?" She held up an odd looking knife. Serrated, there was a colored gauge along the handle.

He shrugged and caught the grin on Leland's face. "What kind of knife is it?"

"It's a warming butter knife," she explained. "Heat transfers from the palm of your hand to the end of it, so you can cut into a cold stick of butter and melt it onto a piece of toast in a jiffy. This is a bargain at eight dollars. They generally cost around thirty."

He grinned. "I'm impressed."

"We have a little of everything here," Leland said dryly. "If there's anything you need, I'm sure we can find it."

A burly man probably in his fifties, Leland was slightly over medium height, with deep set eyes and an air of almost blustery confidence. Miles couldn't see how a drug operation could be operating through here and the guy not know about, or at least suspect, it.

"I'll keep that in mind." He looked down the hall and spotted Keaton coming to relieve him. "See you around."

His undercover shift started and ended an hour earlier than Erin's, so he spent the hour going over everything with Keaton and accompanying him on his first round of the mall.

~

When Erin exited the vision center, she found Miles leaning against the wall near the doorway. He pushed upright. "I think you should stay in Ozark with your parents again tonight."

She didn't bother to argue as he escorted her to the parking lot and to her car. "I'll be right behind you," he said once she was behind the wheel. He hurried to his own vehicle just down the lot from her.

Erin pulled the door shut and inserted a key in the ignition. As she raised her head, in the rearview mirror she saw a car pull from a spot near the edge of the lot. Suddenly the car's engine revved, and it came speeding across the lot. As it zoomed past her, a bullet slammed through her driver's door window, shattering it and thudding into the opposite door frame.

Erin's head exploded as a spray of glass and metal fragments hit her back and neck. The car's tires screeched, and it sped away as she slumped behind the wheel.

A heartbeat passed. And then another.

The door swung open, and Miles was there. "Were you hit? Are you all right?"

Shaky and nauseous, she raised her head. Hot air swept over her from the shattered side window. She swiped blood from her cheek. "I'm okay," she said, easing upright, her body shaking. "Is he gone?"

"Yes. I called for backup."

She realized Miles had come to her aid rather than getting in his truck and pursuing the shooter. She ran a hand over her neck and wiped away fragments of glass.

I'm alive. Thank you, God.

Sirens sounded, and moments later two cruisers veered into the parking lot.

After answering questions and convincing Miles and the other officers that she didn't need to be taken to the hospital, Erin gave Miles a weary smile of resignation. "Yes, I know you want me to go stay with my parents."

"Or in a motel," he bargained.

"I'll call a repair shop to come get my car. Then I'll go to my parents. I had promised to bring Mom up here in the morning so she can do some Saturday shopping at the mall. I could drive their car, which wouldn't be recognizable to whoever is after me."

"No, we'll do it this way. I'll follow you to the repair shop and then drive you to your parents' house. Then, in the morning, I'll come get you. Keaton will take my guard shift. We're flexible that way," he added, his tone slightly more relaxed. "The Ozark department has agreed to have someone watching you all night, and I'll pick you up in the morning. Let's go."

She wanted to tell him she didn't need all that watching and escorting, but her parents had to be considered. Common sense reigned. "Okay."

"Just so you understand, whoever tried to shoot you meant business. We can't be too careful."

They drove to the repair shop and parked. After talking to the owner, Miles boosted her into the cab of his truck, his hand on her back causing a flutter in her mid-section. When he closed the door and rounded the vehicle, she breathed deeply and scooted to the edge of the seat, trying to slow her heart rate as she buckled the seat belt.

Only after he had delivered to her to her parents' home did she breathe easier. Her dad's gaze followed her through supper preparation, but he didn't question her until they were at the table. "What happened today?"

Erin explained about the shooting, knowing they would sense evasions. They knew about her seeing the shooter at the political rally and would guess the implications.

By the time she finished, Mom's mouth was pursed. "That security guard sure seems to have our back. Is he as handsome as he sounds?"

"Uh, I guess so."

Mom grinned. "That means he is. And the fact that you don't want to gush over him tells me a lot." She didn't elaborate.

"I'm hungry," Erin said, ending the topic.

Saturday morning, she rose early and peeked outside. The squad car she'd seen at two a.m. was still there, but as she was getting dressed at eight-thirty, she heard it drive away. Another took its place, and she knew Miles had arrived.

The July heat was already near stifling as she and her mother climbed into his vehicle. Erin didn't argue when Verna insisted on sitting in the back seat of the extended cab pickup, with Erin in the front. She sneaked peripheral glances at Miles as he drove, each look causing a surge of excitement as she memorized the lines of his face.

When they arrived at the mall, she hopped out quickly and hurried to help Verna down to the parking lot that was already scorching from the sun reflecting off it.

Miles rounded the truck and escorted them to the entrance. Inside, Erin faced him. "We should be fine in here. If you have anything you need to do, people to see, go ahead."

He shook his head. "Remember where you were when that kid grabbed your purse?"

He had a valid point.

"I'll wait in front of each place while you shop."

They browsed through the flea market first, with Miles following not far behind them.

"I love the smells," Verna commented, inhaling as they neared a booth. "Scented candles," she said, taking another whiff. She ended up buying a magnolia blossom candle for current use and a mistletoe one for the holiday season later in the year.

They moved on, with Mom identifying fresh roasted peanuts, spices, and other scents she enjoyed. She sniffed and frowned as she bypassed the tobacco products booth.

They visited a shoe shop next, where Verna bought a pair of sandals. Then, after a stop at a card shop, they arrived at a woman's clothing store.

"I'll hold those for you while you shop," Miles offered, indicating the bags Erin carried.

She handed them over and entered with her mother. They browsed through the racks, with Erin pulling off items that she thought would suit her mother for the wedding her parents planned to attend later in the month. She described each garment while Verna examined them by touch.

"I'd like to try on this one," Verna said of a particular one. A simple dress in a soft pastel blue, it was Erin's favorite of the lot.

"There's a dressing room just to our right. Let's go in there."

Inside it, Erin placed her mother's dress that she removed onto a chair and helped Verna into the new one. As it slid over her shoulders, Verna jerked to a standstill and tilted her head. "What's that?" she asked sharply.

Erin frowned. "I didn't hear anything."

"There was a click. It was soft, but I heard it. It came from there." Verna pointed to a spot above the dressing mirror. She often reminded others that she had no special hearing or smelling abilities, but that she detected more because she was more attentive to those things. "Maybe it was a bug."

Erin followed the line of her mother's pointing finger to the upper edge of the mirror and trailed her fingers along it. Near the top left corner, she felt something that made her visualize a giant beetle.

Carefully she pulled the chair over next to the mirror and stepped onto it. When she eased up onto her tiptoes and peered at the "beetle," she gasped. If she wasn't mistaken, she was looking at a small fiber optic camera about the size of a pencil eraser.

Chapter 6

The expression on Erin's face as she approached him from the back of the store sent a jolt of alarm through Miles. He hurried to meet her.

"I've found something in the dressing room that I think you should see," she said, her voice soft but taut with tension.

"Where's your mother?"

"I left her in the dressing room so no one else could enter." She turned and headed back the way she had come.

Disgust rolled in Miles's gut when he saw the tiny camera Erin showed him. Clutching it, he hopped off the chair he had stood on to reach it. "How did you find it?"

"I heard a click." Verna spoke from the doorway where she stood waiting. "If there's a picture of me on that thing, stomp it," she ordered.

Miles suppressed a grin. He liked the elderly lady's spunk. Erin aimed a wry look at him that made him think such bluntness was common.

"I'll see that the matter is handled properly," he said without inflection, gaining a slight mouth twitch from Erin in spite of the gravity of the matter.

A salesclerk appeared in the doorway next to Verna. "What's going on in here?" she demanded, eyeing the small object Miles held between his fingers.

"These ladies heard a noise and discovered a hidden camera." He pointed to above the mirror. "Do you have any idea how it got up there?"

A hand went over the clerk's mouth, her head moving back and forth. "That's awful. I don't know how or why it's there."

"I think I can guess the why. It's the how that's the question." And he really didn't need this. He was here to stop a drug operation. But his cover as the security guard meant he couldn't ignore other criminal activities going on inside the mall. He would see that Erin and her mother were safely home and then deal with this.

"The local police will have questions for you," he informed the clerk. Then he addressed Erin and her mother. "Are you about done shopping?"

"We're done," Mrs. Stuart said quickly. "I've lost interest in the dress. Take us home."

"Yes, Ma'am." He exchanged a quick smile with Erin.

He escorted them back to his truck and drove them to Ozark. As he pulled to the curb outside the Stuart house, he found himself reluctant to leave Erin, even for the job that had filled his life since losing Shelly.

A couple of snicks sounded behind the seat, making him think Verna had unfolded her cane. He was right. As soon as he turned off the engine, she ordered, "Unlock this door and let me out. You two don't need me back here eavesdropping."

Miles touched the button to release the rear door safety locks. "You're not eavesdropping, and it wouldn't matter if you were."

"You need your privacy. This is my turf. You don't need to see me to the door. But you can watch me if it'll make you feel better." She slammed the door and headed up the sidewalk.

"I guess she told me," he said, chuckling as he watched Verna's progress, the cane moving slightly back and forth before her. Then he looked back at the attractive woman in front of him. That proud tilt of her head. Her shoulders squared in an attitude of taking on the world.

When a lock of her honey-blond hair escaped its clip as she opened the passenger door, he wanted to reach out and touch the strands, keep her there with him. But sanity returned just as his hand began to inch toward her. An air of electricity hummed between them. "I see a cruiser coming up the street," he said, gathering his composure.

He exited the truck and walked Erin to the house. "Please be careful," he said at the door.

She gave him a slight nod and hurried inside.

On his way back to the mall, Miles chided himself. He had to see that Erin was protected, but he couldn't afford to be distracted by her. His brain knew that, but he found her too appealing to ignore. He had to keep his mind on business, not forget that his primary objective was to bring down a drug ring and identify the mastermind behind it.

Over the next two hours, he visited businesses that had changing rooms or tanning salons—and found more cameras. Did Freddy have any part in this? He sure hoped not.

Miles reported his findings. Then he showed him the devices when the man showed up minutes later. After giving a full update, he called Jed Parker.

"Help that detective any way you can, but focus on the drug operation," his boss instructed. "They're separate cases."

But are they run by the same person or persons? Miles wondered without voicing the question to his superior.

~

Erin drove her parents to church the next morning in their car. Miles followed them, having replaced the police cruiser that had been parked outside the house during the night.

"We'll go on and sit with our friends," Mom said at the doorway. "You look after your officer friend."

Erin rolled her eyes at Miles, who had joined them in the parking lot. She didn't want her mother's not-so-subtle attempt at matchmaking to embarrass him. "Sorry about that," she mouthed softly.

He grinned. "Don't be. I'm flattered. Do you mind sitting in the back?"

He didn't say it, but she figured he preferred that in case he, or they, had to leave unexpectedly. The weight of the unsolved cases, plus guarding her, had to wear on him.

She tried to focus on the sermon, but having Miles beside her made it hard. When the service ended, they went outside and waited on the steps for her parents.

"We usually eat at a restaurant on Sundays. Will you let us feed you?" Everett asked Miles when he and Verna joined them.

The invitation seemed to surprise Miles, but he didn't immediately decline. "I'd like that," he said when Erin smiled and nodded that he should.

After a pleasant meal at a steak house, they returned to her parents' home. Another police cruiser was just pulling to the curb, leading Erin to think Miles had notified the Ozark department of their return. He waved and drove away.

Monday morning Erin was again followed to work by a cruiser, this time one from Springfield, and was met by Miles in the mall parking lot. The first thing she noted as they entered the shopping complex was Freddy with a couple of guys she didn't know. When he recognized her and Miles, he quickly stuffed his camera inside the pocket of his baggy shorts.

"In case you're wondering," Miles said softly, "those two young men with our friend Freddy are known for petty crimes."

Erin made a beeline for Freddy. "What are you doing?" she demanded in a near hiss, placing a hand on his arm to lead him away.

"What do you mean?" he asked as they walked toward her office. Miles had dropped back to give them privacy, which Erin appreciated.

"I mean you're out here with guys who have history with the police—and I assume taking more pictures. Why?"

He gave her a defensive scowl. "I'm just taking pictures. It's something I like to do. And Jack and Dooley are my friends."

"Well, you need to be careful about letting your friends lead you into trouble."

"Oh, I won't," he assured her. "I'm just hanging out until I have to go to work. That's in a half hour. I should probably go put on my uniform shirt."

She breathed a breath of relief as he veered toward the stairs. "Okay. I'll see you around."

"I'm going to call and check on my car," she told Miles as he caught up to her.

He nodded. "If it's ready this afternoon, we can swing by on your way home and get it."

"By home, do you mean *my* home? I can't stay with my parents indefinitely," she added when he paused at her office door.

"I'll let you know this afternoon, after I've talked to some people."

Accepting that as a tentative concession, she gave him a nod and unlocked the door, having arrived before Lydia for a change.

The morning passed quickly. At lunch time, Erin slipped out for a couple of tacos rather than ordering something from the food mart and likely having it delivered by Freddy. When she spotted Miles patrolling the hall, she figured he had been keeping an eye on her complex unit and seen her leave it. She shot a look of acknowledgment at him and finished eating.

Rather than return to her office immediately, she strolled to the flea market, not sure why she felt drawn to it. As she moved past tables and booths, she took more interest in the surroundings than usual, paying close attention to the types of items sold there. She also studied the vendors. She recognized the owner, Leland Zink, at a booth talking to a vendor. Their manner seemed casual, nothing furtive or suspicious about them or their surroundings.

The list she had copied from that flash drive file came to mind. Could those silly names be Bike's cutesy way of identifying which booth operators were dealing drugs? The more she thought about it, the more she thought it was possible. But there were so many sellers in here. How in the world did she guess which ones the names meant?

Her gaze skimmed over the huge area, trying to figure how that list could relate. The only booth she could make connect to anything on that list was Wee Duds. Duds were clothes, and wee meant tiny. Together they added up to baby clothes. She searched for such a booth. And found one. The woman sitting at the table with stacks of infant garments looked to be in her thirties, lines of weariness bracketing her eyes.

What about the letters following the silly names? Erin took the list from her purse and glanced at it, as if checking her shopping list. The thing that struck her was the order. M, W, F, S. They fit the order of the days of the week. Could that mean that the drugs were sold in different locations on different days?

As she pondered the idea, her phone rang. Seeing that it was the car repair shop returning the call she had made earlier, she answered quickly. "Your car's ready to be picked up any time," the shop owner informed her.

"I'm at work. I'll try to come for it at the end of my workday. How late will you be open?"

"Until six."

"I'm done at five. If I can't make it for any reason, I'll call you."

When the call ended, she noted the time and hurried back to her office.

~

Miles hadn't consulted God much since losing his wife, but yesterday's church service lingered in his mind. Church had been a haven for him, a place where Shelly had taken him and introduced him to Christian fellowship. He had grown to love being there and had become a Christian, regardless of the fact that his parents didn't share his faith.

When they opposed his decision to marry Shelly, knowing she couldn't live much longer, a barrier had been erected between them. He had loved Shelly and wanted to spend whatever time he could with her. She had wanted that, too. He didn't regret what he had done, but he still ached from the loss of her.

His parents had tried to mend their bridges, but their relationship remained strained. He had ignored it, or tried to, for a long time now. Yesterday's message about forgiveness had made him take a hard look at himself. Maybe it was time to put the past behind him, forgive them and make an honest effort to reestablish their relationship. And pray that God would work in the hearts of his parents.

"Have you found anything on that sports booth vendor?"

Keaton's question snapped his attention back to the list they had compiled of all the vendors, their names and what products they sold in the flea market. Miles was on duty, but Keaton had arrived early to go over the case with him before the shift change. They had been working their way through the list, searching for anything in vendor backgrounds that would suggest drug dealing.

"There are two that I'm trying to find out more about. I'm not sure why, but I get an uneasy feeling around them."

Keaton shifted his attention from the computer to Miles. He sat at the security office desk while Miles occupied a chair facing him. "Which ones?"

"That vendor selling household cleaning supplies near the south corner of the market, and the sports booth. I think I remember seeing Bike near those booths in the days before he pulled that theft caper and went into hiding."

Keaton nodded. "Why don't I go out there and chat with those two while you concentrate on researching them?"

"I like the idea. Let's touch base before I escort Erin home."

Keaton grinned. "It's a real hardship looking after the doctor, huh?"

Miles shrugged, not bothering to deny anything. "She needs protection." He turned to the computer, ending the subject.

A half hour later, Keaton returned.

"What have you found?" Miles asked.

"Not a lot. The sports booth operator is a woman with teenage sons. She seemed open and innocent enough, but finding that a teenage son sometimes works the booth for her after school bothers me. The cleaning supplies guy was a high school drop-out, but he's survived reasonably well. Has an address in a nice neighborhood, a wife, and a couple of kids."

"No police record?"

Keaton perched on the edge of the desk. "He's clean on the surface, but when I hinted that the police are looking for Bike, and that Bike had been seen hanging around that booth, he admitted that Bike told him he had information he planned to use to blackmail someone. The guy insists he doesn't know who Bike meant to blackmail. I need to get back out there."

When Keaton was gone, Miles met Erin and escorted her to his truck. As he pulled out of the parking lot, she cleared her throat. "I've been thinking."

He glanced over at her. "What about?"

"The list on that flash drive."

His interest piqued. "I'd love to hear those thoughts."

"Well," she said slowly, as if gathering her thoughts, "I was looking over the market, trying to see how those silly names on Bike's list could be his cutesy nicknames for vendors selling drugs, so others wouldn't know who he meant, and assuming he knew who they were."

He swerved into the center lane to make a left to the repair shop. "I'm all ears."

"Well, I think Wee Duds could refer to the children's clothing booth. And I think the letter M could possibly represent Monday. The order of the letters matches the days of the week," she explained, as if reaffirming her theory.

He nodded while steering off the thoroughfare. "So you think that vendor could be dealing on Mondays, meaning others have assigned days as well. Having business conducted at different locations at different times sounds smart, I have to admit. Do you have theories as to what booths the other names could represent?"

"No, that's as far as I had gotten when the mechanic called to say my car is ready. Then I had to go back to the office for my next appointment."

He pulled into a parking lot. "It looks like your car is waiting for you."

After following her home, Miles called Keaton and shared her thinking.

"I'll follow that line of reasoning," he said brusquely, "but right now I'm on my way to a store where a shoplifter has been caught."

~

"Whatcha think?" Lydia tipped her head to one side and then the other, displaying her latest choice in eyewear, vintage cat-eye frames this time.

Erin snickered under her breath at her assistant's flair for the dramatic, doubting the value of her modeling as advertising.

Lydia grinned and crossed her arms over her chest, her jovial expression morphing to studious. "You look good in the company of that new security guard. Are you sure there isn't more going on between you two than just police protection?"

Unsure exactly how to assess her feelings for Miles, or how to deny that there were any, Erin shook her head and picked up the file lying on Lydia's desk. "I should look at this before Mrs. Phillips arrives."

"She's not due for another ten minutes, but she'll arrive at the last second and then complain if she has to wait more than two minutes."

Erin grinned, but didn't confirm the lady's prickly temperament. "The sooner we get her in, the sooner she'll be done."

"And out," Lydia added as Erin headed back to her office.

Erin stared at the patient record without really seeing it, her mind reverting of its own will to Miles. She couldn't figure out why she was so attracted to him, a man so different from her dad.

She had a business to run. Debts to pay. Aging parents to look after.

She hadn't been a total recluse throughout her life. She had been social to a point, but not focused on finding the kind of intimate relationships to which most of her friends, classmates and associates aspired. She had attempted it once, with Jeff during college, because he'd been charming and fun. And it had seemed the thing expected of her. When it hadn't worked out, she hadn't been all that heartbroken, just upset that she had set herself up for failure. Since then, she had shied away from men, unwilling to open herself to rejection or hurt.

Shaking off the thoughts, Erin set to work. When she left work at five o'clock, she again found Miles outside her doorway. As they walked to the building exit, two ladies offered them campaign buttons supporting Senator Fielder.

"It doesn't go well with my uniform," Miles declined.

Erin also passed, not prone to wear political buttons for anyone. "Do you think Fielder will win reelection?" Miles asked as he pushed the door open for them to exit.

"He probably will. Incumbency garners a lot of automatic votes."

"Unless the incumbent has been involved in a scandal," he qualified.

"There is that. But that hasn't happened to Fielder."

As they walked toward the employee parking area, Erin glanced across the lot and spotted a shadow at the far side of her car that made her breath catch. Someone was lurking there.

"I see him," Miles said, landing a hand on her shoulder. "Stay here."

Erin watched Miles run in a low crouch, circling around to the back of her car. Then he broke into a dead run, rounded the rear of the car and tackled the intruder.

Erin ran toward them, unable to stand and watch. As she circled the car, Miles and the other man scuffled on the ground. The sudden flash of a gun sent her heart into overdrive.

She halted, wanting to help but realizing she shouldn't distract Miles. Helplessly, she watched the man with dark glasses land a hard blow on Miles's head with his gun.

Momentarily stunned, Miles lost his grip on his opponent, and the guy jumped to his feet. He took off across the parking lot, but then he slowed, turned and fired his gun.

The impact of the bullet sent a spray of asphalt fragments over Miles's prone body.

Erin slid to her knees, unmindful of damage to her white slacks, and grasped his shoulder. "Are you okay?"

"Yeah," Miles said in a half groan. "But not okay enough to catch him. My head's scrambled."

She winced. "Should I call an ambulance?"

"No." He extended a hand, which she grasped and held tightly while he levered himself to a sitting position. Then he released her hand and pushed to his knees. As he stood, he traced a finger over the knot on his forehead.

"Should I call the police?"

He started to nod, but stopped, blinking in pain. "Yes."

While dialing, she dug her phone and keys from her purse and clicked the button to unlock her car door. "You need off your feet. Sit." She pointed at the passenger seat.

Miles eased onto it and listened while she reported the incident. When she disconnected, she leaned closer to study his eyes and make sure they were focusing.

"I have a hard head," he said, managing a semblance of a smirk. "Do you have any idea who that was?"

"I don't know, but the dark glasses and body build remind me of the guy I saw after the shooting at that rally. The only thing I'm positive about is that it wasn't my would-be purse snatcher, seeing that he's dead. Of course, it could have been Bike, but I don't think so."

Miles gave her a grim look. "I think your first guess is right. Not only was he wearing the dark glasses, but I think the hair was a wig. It looked like the one worn by the guy in the surveillance footage, the guy who shot Dexter Thornton. And I don't think he was trying to break into your car. I think he meant to kill you."

She did, too. The thought chilled her.

Sirens sounded, and the police arrived moments later.

After explaining what had happened and answering their questions, Erin and Miles were told they could leave.

Miles had been advised to seek medical attention, but insisted he was okay.

"Will you at least let me call a friend and let her take a look at you? She's the director of an in-home health center. Please," she added before Miles could refuse.

His eyes narrowed. "You don't play fair."

She smiled, some of the tension oozing from her. If he could make that light a comeback, his injuries surely weren't too serious.

Chapter 7

Miles stared at Erin's pretty face, its pleasant expression jabbing at him. He battled the sensation. Her direct manner was similar to Shelly's. Why he would think of his wife now eluded him. He had learned to deal with the loss and made his job his life. He couldn't let anything sidetrack him, no matter how gutsy Erin was or how much admiration she stirred in him. He had to shut down a drug operation.

He could let her call her friend, though. "Okay."

Her eyes rounded in surprise at his easy capitulation, but she grabbed her phone and made the call. "We can," she said before disconnecting. "She hasn't left work yet."

"We can what?"

"Go to her workplace. I'll take you and then bring you back for your truck."

Since it meant riding with her rather than following her, he offered no argument.

Minutes later they arrived at the health center and were met at the entrance by a short, pleasant faced redhead who was just slipping a white lab coat over her black tee shirt dress. "Come with me," she instructed after being introduced as Ginger Brewer, a former EMT who had switched to a job with better working hours.

They followed her into an employee break room where his bruised head was checked and rated nasty. He was given an ice pack and the cut on his forehead covered with a Band-Aid.

"Do you want some pain medication to relieve the pounding in your skull?"

"I'd gulp a couple of Tylenol if you have some handy," he said, realizing the woman had read his expression.

She smiled. "It's a deal."

As soon as the pills had been delivered and swallowed, he thanked the woman and told Erin he was ready to leave.

The ride back to the mall parking lot didn't do anything positive for his headache, but he counted on the pills kicking in soon. He leaned back in the seat and closed his eyes. When Erin pulled up beside his truck and stopped, he opened his eyes but didn't sit up yet.

"I've been thinking about that list," he said without moving.

Erin faced him. "You mean the one in Bike's flash drive?"

"Uh huh. I think you made a good guess on Wee Duds meaning baby clothes. And if you're right about the letter representing the day that vendor is selling drugs, that would be Monday. I'll be watching all booths with baby clothes extra close Monday."

"That's good to know."

He pushed upright in the seat, the pain in his head beginning to ease. "I think *Ringer* could be a cutesy nickname for telephones."

She nodded agreement. "And the letter after that one is F. So phone vendors could be dealing on Fridays."

"You've apparently memorized the list. Yes, that's what I was thinking. So I'll concentrate on any vendors with phones in their booths on Friday."

As he finished speaking, his cell phone rang. He pulled it from his belt and looked at the screen. It was the Branson police detective. "Jarrett here."

"A body has been found on our turf that I think is of interest to you."

"Male or female?"

"Male. And we've already identified him as Harley Davis. I believe that's the name you mentioned as your mall thief, and I thought you'd like to be informed."

"Thanks. You're right. Where was he found?"

"In the Lakeside Forest Wilderness Area."

"I'd like to drive down and see the scene. How do I find you?"

The detective gave him directions. "We're in the woods behind the pavilion."

"I'm on my way."

When he disconnected, he met Erin's apprehensive expression.

"What's wrong?"

"Bike is dead." He regretted his bluntness when she gasped, her face whitening. She was visibly shaken, but he hadn't known any soft way of stating the hard fact. "I have to go."

"Where?"

He told her what the Branson detective had told him. "I need to get down there."

"I can drive."

His thoughts whirled. He needed to escort her home. He couldn't go off and leave her. But he had to get to that crime scene. Taking her with him was stupid. An idea popped into his head. "No, I can drive. We'll take my truck."

She grabbed her purse and shot out of the car. He had to run to catch up with her.

"I'll drop you at your parents' house on my way down there," he said while they buckled their seat belts.

Her head whipped around. "You'll do no such thing. We're in this together now, and you need me along in case your head gets to hurting so much you can't drive."

Recognizing when he was defeated, he programmed the GPS and hit the road, driving the speed limit and weaving through the tourist traffic that had peaked. They soon arrived at the park entrance. There was a large wooden log archway over it and an ornamental iron gate with a decorative stone veneer.

A nature playground and pavilion stood nearby. Police cars occupied the area by the pavilion. He parked nearby and exited quickly.

When he showed his badge, they were allowed past the crime scene tape to join the detective. Deputies could be heard back in the trees. It took a couple of minutes to reach them.

The prone body at their feet lay face up, his baggy shorts and tee shirt blood stained. The Branson detective shook his head. "Shot point blank through the temple," he muttered.

It was Bike. No doubt about it. "How long has he been dead?"

"The medical examiner will have to determine that, but from the looks of him I'd guess a week or so. The only reason no one found him sooner is because he had been back here in the trees and covered by a pile of tree limbs and debris. A pair of campers out looking for firewood found him."

Miles thought back over the past few days. "So he was killed soon after breaking into the jewelry store and invading Miss Stuart's house in Springfield. That was before the guy who tried to take her purse was killed. I'm guessing they were both killed over the same thing."

"Continue," the detective said when he paused.

"Bike was trying to recover a flash drive he lost, probably ordered to do so. When he failed, he was killed to keep him from revealing who he was trying to blackmail.

Then another thug was sent to recover it. He also failed and was killed to keep him silent. Whoever was giving the orders apparently has a violent temper. What I don't get is if, or how, any of it relates to my drug case, other than the fact that my undercover role had me chasing Bike for a theft."

"I don't know either," the detective said, "but my gut says they're connected, and your doctor here has become a target. I figure whatever is going on up there in Springfield reaches down here. So we need to work together."

Miles nodded. "I agree."

"I think by now they know I've found the flash drive and given it to you," Erin interjected.

"You're probably right," Miles agreed. "But you're still a target." People involved in this case were dying. And he couldn't relax knowing that.

~

After another restless night, Erin woke with the sensation that something had to give. She couldn't spend her days under guard indefinitely. She had to be proactive.

With that in mind, she followed routine and spent her morning seeing patients. But at lunch time she left the office to browse the flea market, knowing that Miles was nearby.

It worried her that a killer thought she could identify him. She wished she could. Nothing would suit her more than to be able to pick him out of a lineup or photo album and help the police nail him. But she couldn't. All she could think to do at this point was what Miles had said he meant to do, look for booths that sold baby clothes or telephones.

Joining the flow of shoppers, she wandered through the aisles and stopped at a craft booth that had a stack of colorful throw blankets on display, thinking her mom would like one. Verna was cold natured and liked to cover her lap for warmth when Dad turned the air conditioner too high for her.

After selecting a lightweight fleecy one, Erin paid for it and glanced around while the vendor wrapped and taped the package. Spotting a rack of summer clothing, she set the package on the end of the table while she browsed through the rack of tunic tops.

Not finding anything that particularly appealed to her, she picked up her package and returned to work. At five o'clock she gathered her purse and the package and accompanied Lydia out of the office. As she locked the door behind them, she spotted Miles coming up the hall to meet her. He said hello to Lydia, who then went on ahead of them.

"I can't stop thinking about that list of names," Erin said once it was just the two of them, staring over at the flea market as they walked past it. She had started toward the exit when a particular sign caught her eye. She skated to a halt, focusing on it as her brain started clanging. "Books!" she whispered in near excitement

Miles stopped beside her. "What about books?"

"Bookworms read them."

Their gazes locked. "I think you could have something there."

"Worm had me thinking of fishing bait or computer malware, when it could be as simple as books," she repeated in bemusement.

"Bike may have had some disdain for books," Miles theorized with a shrug. "So, yes, I think that could have been a sarcastic title. And the letter following that title was …"

"S," she supplied when he hesitated. "So a book vendor could be a Saturday dealer."

"That covers three names of the four on that list. What about Old Nag?"

She shook her head. "That one still has me stumped. It sounds like there was someone he didn't like, but the question of who leaves me clueless."

"Me, too." He headed on to the exit.

Once Erin was in her car, she drove off the parking lot, Miles's truck visible in her rearview mirror. The man drew her to him in a way no other had ever done, even Jeff.

As she cruised into the next lane, Erin was lulled into a sense of calm. But then she noticed a big truck had moved into the center lane and was keeping pace with Miles. It was black with a chrome grill that glinted in the still bright sunlight, and it was picking up speed.

Suddenly it shot forward and pulled alongside her. The next thing she felt was the impact of it sideswiping her. She fought to keep a grip on the wheel, but her car veered off the road into the ditch, bounced over the rough terrain and came to a sudden stop that jolted her head forward against the steering wheel.

The next thing she knew, her passenger door was jerked open. An arm reached in and snatched the package beside her on the seat. Then the person was gone, the car door left swinging on its hinges.

While Erin was still struggling to clear her head, the driver's door was jerked open. "Are you okay?" Miles asked, his gaze raking over her in concern. It flashed through her mind that he had come to her aid rather than going after the person who had hit her.

"I will be in a few more seconds," she assured him breathlessly.

"Another car cut in front of me," Miles explained needlessly. "The guy in the truck had made it down here and was heading back to his vehicle by the time I could get stopped. I was afraid he had come down here to kill you."

Erin raised her head. "He didn't hurt me, other than running me off the road. He just grabbed the package I had sitting there." She pointed at the empty passenger seat.

"So long as you're okay, that's all that matters. Can you stand?"

"I think so." As she eased out of the car on unsteady legs, strong arms came around her in welcome support.

Miles turned her to face him. Then he took a long breath and gave her a lopsided grin. "I believe we now have matching knots on our heads. Let's get you to a doctor."

"No, I'm fine. I'll take some Tylenol when I get home."

Mention of home made her look over at her car. The rear door had a huge dent in it and there was a streak of damage from the sideswipe. "It looks like I need a tow truck and a ride home."

"Let's wait in my truck for it to be hauled to …where?"

"I'll call Rick, the guy who worked on it earlier. He'll tow it and fix the damage. My insurance company isn't going to be happy about this."

She let him get her purse and assist her up the incline to his truck. Then, while she called Rick, he dialed the police.

It was an hour later when she was finally told she could leave.

~

Miles wanted to take Erin home, but she insisted on knowing what he was going to do later. When he admitted he was going back to the mall to view surveillance footage, she faced him across the seat of his truck. "I want to see it with you."

As he thought about it, keeping her with him seemed the best way to protect her. Watching the tow truck pull her car onto the road, he called Keaton.

"I want to look at surveillance footage. Will you have it set up when we get there? I'll explain when I arrive. Thanks," he said when his partner said he'd have it ready.

When the three of them met at the office, Miles explained what had transpired on the highway and found seats before the flat screen. Miles stared at the image on the screen when Erin picked up her package and walked away. "Back it up," he said when Keaton pushed Pause.

He reversed it.

"There." Miles pointed at where Erin's hand reached for her package. "Can you enlarge it?"

As he did, Erin gasped. Barely visible was another package of similar size and shape. "I picked up the wrong one. Oh, I feel dreadful. It was my fault."

"You didn't do it deliberately," Miles said, wanting to soothe her distress. "But maybe it's a break for us. Whatever was in the one you took was important enough for someone to run you off the road to recover it."

Her eyes widened. "Drugs?"

"Maybe." He leaned forward to study the picture some more. "Who's that?" He pointed at a girl with her back to Erin. Long dark hair fell down her back.

Erin shook her head. "I don't know."

"I don't know either," Keaton said, which wasn't surprising. Like Miles, he had only been around since being assigned this case.

"Will you get the best shot of her that you can? Then we can show it around and see if anyone recognizes her."

Keaton complied and printed two copies. Then he glanced at Erin and printed a third for her.

Miles nodded approval. "You might get lucky and spot her," he said to Erin. Then he glanced at his watch. "Most of the vendors have shut down for the evening. Can you come a little early in the morning and take me to visit that booth where you bought your Mom's gift?"

She nodded. "I can do that."

As Miles took Erin home, he tried to ignore his pretty passenger. Her eyes sparkled beneath the bump on her forehead, while her hair caught the light of the lowering sun and reflected subtle highlights. But there was more to her than just physical beauty. She was special. A longing held him in its grasp, so powerful it stole his breath.

His gut clenched. He didn't do serious. He didn't do romance. That was a perilous path he couldn't risk again. He couldn't handle another round of that kind of loss. When this case was resolved, he would move on to another one, another location. No ties. No heartache.

"I'll pick you up in the morning," he said as he pulled to the curb at Erin's house. She simply nodded, scooted out of his truck and headed to the door.

The next morning, she was ready when he arrived and waved at the officer who had been parked there through the early morning hours. He drove to the mall quickly, the city traffic not too heavy yet. Inside, they went directly to the booth where Erin had made that purchase.

She took the lead, marching up to the booth and greeting the middle-aged lady vendor. "Good morning," she said pleasantly. "I was here yesterday and purchased a throw blanket for my mother. Surveillance footage shows that there were two packages on this table, so I must have inadvertently taken the wrong one. On the way home, someone ran me off the road and took the package from my car. Do you by chance still have my package here?"

The woman's brow furrowed in puzzlement. Then her expression brightened. "Yes, as a matter of fact, there was a package left here yesterday. Let me see if I can find it."

Miles noticed that Erin didn't say how she was run down or how the package was taken. And this woman seemed genuinely perplexed. He watched her bend over and rummage around beneath the table for a couple of minutes.

When her head popped back up, she was smiling and holding up a package. "Is this it?"

Erin took it, tore the wrapping paper open at one end of the package and peeked at the contents. "Yes, that's it. Thank you."

"I'm sorry for the mix-up," the woman apologized.

Miles took the surveillance photo from his wallet and held it before her. "Do you recognize the girl standing next to Dr. Stuart?"

The woman peered at the picture for several moments, squinting in concentration. Then she shook her head. "Not without seeing her face. I'm sorry."

He tucked the picture back in his wallet and thanked her.

As he and Erin started to walk away, Erin came to a sudden halt, staring at the booth next to the one they had just left. He thought he could hear the wheels of her brain whirring.

She stood there a few more moments and then nudged his arm. "Let's go somewhere private."

He escorted her to the security office. As soon as he closed the door, she pulled out her copy of the surveillance picture and peered at it intensely. Then an exultant smile crossed her face.

"I know who one of the drug dealers is."

He smiled. And waited.

"It's the antique booth next to that craft booth where I bought Mom's blanket. Look at this." She held the picture in front of him.

Miles looked at where her finger pointed.

"Those packages were at the end of that table, but it's shoved right up against the next one. Someone bought something there and set it on the crack between the two tables—probably while paying for it. I didn't notice and took it by mistake while they were busy."

She met his gaze directly. "It fits that fourth item on the list. Old."

He turned that over in his mind. And then he grinned. "Antiques are old things."

She nodded. "Nag." Her grin said she was enjoying her little guessing game with him.

He took the picture from her and stared at it again. "That booth isn't visible here—except the tip end of the table."

"There was an older woman there. And she wore a sour expression. I'm betting Bike had some kind of beef with her and considered her a nag."

He snorted. But he thought she could be right. "And there's a W by that name on the list. That means Wednesday is her day to sell drugs if we're right about the letters. And yesterday was Wednesday. So the woman was dealing, and the customer wasn't careful enough with his package—or was distracted for some reason."

"Maybe price haggling," Erin suggested, opening the door to leave.

~

During a mid-morning break between patients, Erin checked her phone and found a text from Miles.

I'll pick you up at noon for sandwiches and updates in my office. Say yes.

She typed *yes* and sent it.

An hour and a half later, they sat in the tiny security office having chicken sandwiches and iced tea. Miles didn't mention the case until they finished eating.

"I've had no luck getting an ID on the girl in the picture," he said after tossing their paper containers in the trash. "Without her face showing, no one can identify her. But I'll keep showing the picture around."

"What about the antique booth? Have you learned anything about the woman operating it?"

"I did some research. Her name is Harriet Wickham. She's fifty-two years old, and she's a heavy gambler. When I showed her that picture, I'm sure I saw a look of panic flash in her eyes, but she denied knowing who had been at her booth at that time. After leaving her, I hurried in here and watched her on surveillance to see what she would do. She sat down and wrote a note. Then, after taking care of a customer, she took the note up the hall and handed it to the guy at a booth that sells tech items. As soon as she left, he read the note, looked around and left his booth."

"Out of camera range?"

He nodded. "Those two are on my watch list now. I'm going to update Keaton."

"And I'm going back to work," she said as he dialed his partner.

"I was wondering if you'd gotten lost," Lydia said when Erin entered the office.

Her assistant kept close tabs on her, sometimes with what felt a bit like nosiness, but she was capable and did a good job. She also devoted time working with her church's food bank.

"Mrs. Richards is waiting in the exam room."

"Okay, thanks."

The afternoon passed quietly. After Lydia left, Erin gathered her purse and exited the office. She saw Miles down the hallway, coming toward her. The sight of Freddy ambling from the opposite direction made her assume he had worked late at the food mart.

Freddy skidded to an abrupt halt when he spotted Miles.

Erin hurried after him as he turned to walk back the way he had come. "Wait," she said, grasping his arm.

He paused, frowning. "What?"

She pulled the picture from her purse. "I'd like you to look at this picture and tell me if you know that girl." She placed a fingertip on the image.

Freddy's frown deepened, but he studied it for several seconds. "I can't see enough, but she looks familiar. She sure has pretty hair," he added before returning the picture.

"Will you let me know if you get an idea?"

Freddy's head bobbed. Then he took off at a near run.

"I don't think he really considers me a friend," Miles said, walking alongside her to the exit. Just before they reached it, he looked to his left. A young man who was coming down that hallway turned and headed for the exit ahead of them.

"That's the tech vendor I've been watching. I want to talk to him. Wait here."

Miles loped toward after the guy.

The vendor looked back, and when he saw Miles he broke into a run.

Chapter 8

As Miles took off in pursuit, Erin also sprang into motion, not about to be left behind. She ran outside, her gaze darting over the parking lot. Ahead of Miles, the young man had already jumped into a nearby SUV. Within seconds, it roared away.

Erin followed Miles around the side of the building to his truck, trying to catch up to him, but falling behind. Inhaling deeply, she pushed for a burst of speed that got her to the truck just in time to grab the door handle as the engine came to life. She yanked the door open and reached for the handhold inside the vehicle. With a desperate heave, she swung her body into the seat, her purse thumping against her side. As she shut the door, the truck shot forward.

Erin released her purse strap and grabbed the seat belt, trying to keep sight of the fleeing car as she buckled the belt. "Who is he?" She dug her phone from her purse as she spoke.

"His name is Mark Hammond. See if you can find an address for him."

She searched and found one. "He lives the opposite direction, so he's not headed home."

Miles nodded and maneuvered through traffic, edging closer to his quarry.

Erin squinted against the glaring summer sun, watching the SUV exit south onto US 65. "I think he's going to Branson."

Miles swung into the next lane and followed. But the SUV had gained more lead.

Erin kept track of the vehicle as it wove through traffic—all the way to Branson. Then, instead of heading into town, it kept going. "I think he's heading for Rockaway Beach," she said when it veered onto State Road F. The suburb was located about ten miles southwest of Branson in Taney County on the shoreline of the White River.

Miles kept his gaze fixed on the road, gripping the steering wheel tightly and closing the distance between them as it went where she predicted. Then, when the blue SUV whipped onto a side road, he slowed and did likewise. The SUV didn't stop, but sped down the country road and onto an even more secluded road flanked by towering trees and dense foliage.

The narrow lane wound up the hillside where the faint outline of a structure appeared. When the SUV made a sharp turn and disappeared from sight, Miles pulled to the side of the road and parked.

They each scooted out of the truck and met in front of the hood. Then, together, they began hiking through the trees. Any other time, Erin would have been more appreciative of their surroundings. The air was fresh and clear, the proliferation of oaks, hickory and pine trees forming a nature haven.

But the heat was stifling. And thick undergrowth plucked at them as they circled through the woods toward the structure that turned out to be a large sized camp tent sheltered in the trees.

Quietly they edged nearer and saw two more cars parked at the far side of the tent, barely visible. "Do you think this is a portable hideout of the drug dealers you're trying to stop?"

"I'm wondering if that's the case." He stepped over a rotten log, reaching for her hand to assist her.

A sudden crack of gunfire erupted, loud and startling. Miles lunged back across the log, taking her to the ground with him.

~

Miles pressed Erin down, cushioning her as much as he could. He had to get her out of here. If he were alone, he'd find a way to confront this guy. But not with her present. Two guys, he amended when another shot reverberated above their heads.

"Please help us, Lord," came from Erin's lips.

He jumped to his feet, drawing his gun and searching their surroundings. Seeing no one, he tugged at her arm. "We have to get out of here." He should never have allowed her to come. He should have forced her from the truck—or stayed with her. He knew Mark Hammond's identity. He could have found him.

But he wouldn't have found this hideaway.

Another bullet cracked, spitting up a puff of undergrowth and wiping everything from his mind but the fact that he had to get Erin to safety.

He ran, tugging her alongside him. She yelped as she skidded over loose leaves, fighting for balance. He tightened his grip on her arm, hauled her to her feet and charged through the woods.

When they finally arrived back at his truck, her breath was coming in ragged gasps. She blinked up at him as he yanked the passenger door open. He gave her a shove into the seat, slammed the door and raced around to the driver's side.

Some of the tension drained from him as he drove away and headed back north. He debated what to do about Erin. And he had to call his superior.

She solved his quandary. "You need to go back to the mall and touch base with your people, so let's go straight there."

"And when I'm done, we can grab something to eat." The words spilled out of his mouth before he could stop them.

She produced a weak smile, stealing the breath from his lungs. "While you're taking care of your business, I could order pizzas and cold drinks. What do you like on your pizza?"

"Anything. Everything. And a large root beer to drink." He was glad she couldn't hear the rapid pace of his heart.

He drove to the mall and escorted her inside. When they spotted Keaton patrolling the flea market portion of the complex, Miles beckoned for him to follow them. When they met, he led the way to a quiet spot and quickly related what had occurred over the past hour.

"You did the right thing in coming back," Keaton said when Miles finished. "We have nothing solid to charge anyone with, so it's better to not stir the pot anymore at this point."

Miles agreed. "Let's watch that particular booth, see if Hammond shows up to run it."

Keaton scowled. "I'm guessing he won't, but we'll keep surveilling and gathering evidence, paying extra attention to the four booths on that list. We don't want to risk blowing our cover."

Miles nodded. "You go on back to your duties. I'll go to the office and make some calls. Jed and the local police need to be brought up to speed."

Keaton headed back to his post, and Miles and Erin hurried to the tiny security office. By the time he had his calls made, their pizzas had been ordered and a delivery boy arrived at the door with them. Miles hurried to pay the bill before Erin could.

She put her purse back on the desk. "I owe you a meal."

He grinned. "I've already had a meal at your dad's expense."

"Are you getting discouraged?" she asked, dragging the spare chair up to the desk as he placed the pizza boxes in the center.

"A little," he admitted. "But we don't want to make any arrests too soon."

"You want to nail whoever's behind the operation, not just a couple of underlings."

"That's right." He sat behind the desk, and they each bowed their heads for a moment of silent thanks.

As a preacher's daughter, he had no doubt Erin would pray before a meal. He had grown lax about such things since losing Shelly. He wasn't so angry or disillusioned that he denied the existence of God. He just didn't seek Him out the way he had in the years after becoming a Christian. He had drifted from that closeness with his maker. Being back in church Sunday had been comforting. He needed to make it a regular practice again. Spend time around other Christians. Put God back in control of his life.

The thought sent encouragement coursing through him.

Being with Erin, seeing how she and her family lived, offered him a sense of wholeness he hadn't felt since Shelly's death. The hole left by that had seemed a lifelong sentence, but now new emotions, spurred by new people, were beginning to fill him with new hope for the future.

He needed to trust God to lead.

"How long have you been a DEA agent?" Erin asked, bringing his attention back to the moment.

"Not all that long," he admitted. "I applied right after college graduation, but I hadn't entered college immediately after high school."

He took a sip of root beer, pulling himself together. "I wanted to go into law enforcement, but I couldn't leave Shelly. So I took a job with the local police department. They sometimes hire young rookies with clean records," he added with a shrug. "The chief was my buddy's dad."

She smiled. "He understood about your wife."

"Yeah, he knew. The doctor said Shelly was too weak to have children, so we didn't. After her death, I enrolled in college and then applied to become an agent. I've been one for six years." He reached for a slice of pizza.

They ate quickly and silently, each lost in thought. When they finished, he tossed the empty boxes and debris in the trash, and they left the office.

When he drove up in front of her parents' house in Ozark, Erin reached for the door handle, and he hopped out of the truck to accompany her. When they arrived at the door, he reached over and cupped her cheek, turning her face toward him. And the next thing he knew, he had bent his head and kissed her.

When he pulled away, he struggled for words. It had felt so right. "I never expected to feel such a kinship with anyone again."

Erin smiled at him. "It's just as unexpected for me."

"Lock your doors," he cautioned, backing away. He glanced over at the patrol car just pulling to the curb.

She nodded and stepped inside.

Friday morning, Miles wasn't surprised at entering the mall and seeing Mark Hammond's booth closed. While escorting Erin to her office, he eyed the sports and cleaning supplies booths, wondering what those vendors knew about Hammond. He was still pondering it as he went to relieve Keaton from duty.

Then he did a walk-through of the complex. After stopping for brief chats at the sports and cleaning supplies booths, he felt a measure of reassurance that those two vendors were legit.

As he headed back toward the entrance, his phone rang. It was Keaton. "Yeah."

"On the way to my truck to leave, a kid came running over to me and said there was somebody hurt over by the building. He led me around to the rear entrance, and I found a guy who has been severely beaten. He says his name is Freddy."

"I'm on my way." Miles did an about face and hurried to the rear of the mall. When he arrived, he found Keaton kneeling next to Freddy, who was sitting on the ground with his knees drawn up, his head leaning forward on them.

Miles squatted next to Freddy while asking Keaton, "Have you called an ambulance?"

Freddy looked up. "I told him I don't need one." One eye was blackened and swollen nearly shut. His mouth was bloody, and there was a cut on his cheek, another on his hand. From the looks of him, Miles surmised there were bruises all over his body.

"Who did this to you, Freddy?"

"I don't know," he mumbled.

"Do you mean you didn't recognize them, or were they dressed so you couldn't tell who they were?"

"They wore something over their faces."

Miles nodded and pointed in a silent signal for Keaton to move to the other side of Freddy while he moved to the shoulder closest to him. Together they hoisted the young man to his feet. "We'll take you to the office where we can talk privately," he explained to Freddy. People had gathered to watch, and the guy was already rattled. This had the taste of something the general public didn't need to hear and see.

They assisted Freddy to the security office and seated him in a chair. Then Keaton got their first aid kit and cleaned and bandaged the man's cuts.

"Now can you tell us what happened?" Miles asked when they were finished, and Freddy had been given a cold cup of water and had a little time to think.

Freddy's eyes focused on them in a blank stare. "I'm not sure."

"How did you end up at the back of the building?" Keaton asked.

Freddy pondered for several moments and wagged a finger in the air. "I was in the hall, on my way to work, and someone came up behind me. He said there was a girl back there that wanted to talk to me."

"So you went to see her."

He nodded. "But when I went out the door, two guys jumped me and started beating me."

"Why would they do that?"

Bewilderment etched his face. "I don't know."

"Didn't they say anything?" Keaton asked.

"They said I called the cops about the cameras, or somethin' like that. It didn't make sense."

"I assume you told them you didn't do it," Miles said, thinking this must mean that Freddy really wasn't involved in the porn. It was a relief, but it also meant this beating was related to that case, one that belonged to the local police department.

Freddy's hand went over his face, fear radiating from his eyes. "They said they'd beat me more if I told anyone."

"They won't hurt you again," Keaton assured him. "They're going to be stopped. And we're going to keep our eye on you to be sure you're safe."

That seemed to calm him some, but not completely.

Keaton pulled out his phone. "I'm calling the local police."

Miles focused on Freddy. "Do you need to go home?"

Freddy shook his head. "I can work. I need to. And I need to hurry. I'm late."

"I'll go with you and explain things to your boss. I'll also tell him you'll need to talk to the police when they get here."

Chapter 9

Not wanting to order lunch or venture out today, Erin had brought a sandwich. They kept sodas in the small boxy refrigerator in the supply room. While eating at her desk, she relished the quiet. Lydia had left at noon as usual and would return at one.

At the end of the day, Erin met Miles, as had become their pattern.

"Do you know for sure how Bike fit into things?" she asked once they were inside his truck. "Was he involved in the porn and drug operations, or just the drug dealing?"

"I think he was involved in the drug trade, probably as a gofer or message carrier. And in the process of that he saw and heard a lot. Then he got greedy and decided on blackmail."

"So you think the porn is a separate racket, probably making and selling videos?"

He started the engine and looked over his shoulder to back out of the parking spot. "That's my gut feeling. It's the local cops' case, so I've kept them informed about what we've found. The detective isn't sure, but he thinks Leland is using teen thugs to get pictures for him. The last time I talked to him, he said he was getting ready to take Leland in for questioning.”

“What about the lady who runs the antiques booth?”

He looked both ways and pulled into the street before answering. “I’ve done some more research on Mrs. Wickham. She’s divorced, with two grown children who live in different states. She used to work in a Reno casino, but left after a shooting incident. The casino people suspected her of involvement, but they couldn’t prove it. She returned to Missouri. Her dad, whose name is Archie Mullins, lives here, and he’s no stranger to law enforcement and jail.”

Erin struggled to assimilate all the facts and ramifications. “It sounds like she now ranks high on your list of suspected dealers.”

He pulled out of the parking lot into the street. “I think she is. And I think you’re right about Bike’s list dubbing her as Old Nag. I also think you’re right about her day to deal being Wednesday.”

“Where do you think she gets her stuff?”

He heaved a sigh and changed lanes. “I’m not having any luck finding out who’s bringing in the stuff, or how she hides it. People in the drug trade are clever. They’ve figured out ways to conceal their stock from even the best agents.”

“Can you use K-9 dogs?”

“If we bring dogs into the mall, we’ll blow our cover, and the operation will move to another location. Then we’ll never nail whoever is behind the whole operation.”

“I respect your judgment, as well as your dedication. I’m spending time in prayer for your success. I’ve shared the matter with my parents—who are very discreet—and they’ve added it to their prayer list.”

He gave her a rueful smile. “I’m sure there’s strength in prayer.”

His tone made her think he might have abandoned that surety after losing his wife. Sympathy gripped her heart at his renewal of trust in God. “What do you plan to do next?”

"I'm going back to Rockaway Beach and have a chat with Mr. Mullins, if I can find him."

"Take me with you. I want to go. It'll save you the time of taking me home before you go."

He glanced over at her, his look saying he was measuring her intent. It took several seconds for him to reach a decision. "You can go, but only if you do whatever I tell you."

"You're in charge."

He veered back into the right lane and picked up speed.

"Is meth as big a problem as I've heard?"

He nodded, his face set in a grim expression. "It's ruining more lives and communities in the Ozarks than any other drug. It's such an epidemic that some people use the 417 area code as slang for it."

"I've heard the term 417, but I didn't realize the significance. Are there a lot of meth labs operating in the area?"

"Not as many as there used to be. Locals cooking meth has dropped off, but it's not because law enforcement is finding the labs. It's because the labs have been replaced by people bringing in meth, usually from Mexico, or somewhere south. It's easier to get, better quality and cheaper. So larger amounts are being seized than in the past."

"The drugs are illegal in themselves," he continued, "but they also contribute to other crimes, such as domestic violence, property crimes and theft by people after money, or items they can pawn, in order to buy their drugs."

He reached into his shirt pocket and withdrew a piece of paper. "I jotted down the address I found. Will you program it into the GPS for me?"

"Sure." She took the paper and did the task.

Nearly an hour later, he drove through the main street of the resort town and continued on to where the GPS directed. He turned onto a rural road that headed up a hillside into a forest. As the terrain climbed, the woods became denser and more overgrown each side of the narrow road. The Ozarks were not mountains in the typical sense, but were actually a plateau that had been uplifted and then dissected by streams eroding and down-cutting through the uplifted area.

They spotted a mailbox at the end of a long driveway. The house Miles drove up to at the end of it was rustic to say the least. It looked like it had been there for many years, and it was doubtful it had such amenities as electricity and water.

They exited the truck and walked to the door. Miles knocked.

The door opened to reveal an older man with white hair and bushy eyebrows—and a shotgun cradled in his arm. "What do you want?" he growled.

"Are you Mr. Archie Mullins?"

Dark eyes narrowed, focused on Miles's guard uniform. "So what if I am."

Miles extended a hand, which was ignored. "I'm Miles Jarrett, and I need your help."

The man's lips twisted. "No cop ever wants my help unless it's to land me in jail." He backed away and started to push the door shut.

Erin stepped forward quickly, blocking the door with a hand. "All we want is to talk to you, Mr. Mullins."

"We believe your daughter has a booth in the mall flea market," Miles added quickly. "There have been some incidents, and we're looking for information that will help us guarantee the safety of the businesspeople as well as customers."

The old man's brows pulled together, his jaw tight. "I don't know anything that would help you." With that, he slammed the door.

Erin faced Miles. "You tried."

He shrugged. "It was a bust. Let's get you home."

When they were back in the truck, Erin remained quiet for several minutes, thoughts and images rolling around in her head. "I've seen that man before," she said once she was certain.

Miles darted a glance over at her, and then returned his attention to the highway. "Where?"

"At first I wasn't sure, but after thinking about it, I'm positive I saw him at the mall recently. I don't remember what day it was, but I remember he was talking to Leland, the owner of the flea market."

~

Miles added that tidbit to his conglomerate of facts, thinking it solidified the theory that Leland was behind the drug dealing. Maybe the porn business as well. Research on the man hadn't turned up anything worse than a couple of speeding tickets and some trouble over missed child support payments, but that didn't eliminate him from suspicion. A clever crook could go undetected for a long time—or indefinitely.

He was torn between the undercover drug investigation and the local porn case that was sidetracking him. The police department took responsibility for the porn case, but what if they were being run by the same person?

They had to work in cooperation. And they had been.

Erin was introspectively quiet as he drove, making him think she could be having similar thoughts.

"Will you spend the weekend with your parents?" he asked as they reached the city limits of Ozark.

"I'd be safe enough at home, but I think it will make them feel better if I stay with them," she decided after a few seconds. "I hope I get my car back the first of the week."

"Check on it Monday, and we'll pick it up after work if it's ready."

He drove to her parents' house. When he parked, he shut off the motor and placed a hand on Erin's shoulder. And met eyes so wide and troubled that looking at them shook him.

"Don't worry about bringing trouble to your parents. It'll reassure them to have you in their presence. And you'll be under close watch. The Ozark cops are helping us."

She nodded, her pupils dilating even more.

His gaze traveled over her features one by one—and rested on her mouth. His heart thudded against his chest, disjoined thoughts tumbling through his head. He was crazy to be thinking about kissing her.

She didn't pull away when he traced his fingertips along the edge of her jaw and tucked a strand of hair behind her ear.

The sudden ring of his phone startled them, breaking the tenuous thread between them. He scooted out the door and answered it, noting the ID. "Yeah, Julian," he said as Erin scooted from the truck and went to meet her dad on the porch.

"I worked some magic and got a look at Bike's Facebook Messenger," the tech expert said. "There was a message shortly after that smash and grab and parking lot incident. It said, 'The boss said get it. Or else.'"

"That had to refer to the flash drive. Who sent it?"

"It came from the account of someone by the name of Ronny Kinzer."

Miles made a mental note of the name and started the truck. "I'll see if I can find him. Thanks for the call. I wish the guy had used the boss's name."

Whoever it is, it's someone who shouldn't be crossed, he thought as they ended the call. *Bike made a mistake when he decided on blackmail. He didn't realize how powerful a guy he was going up against. And it got him killed.*

He spent the next two hours running down leads, making calls and driving to the address he finally located for Ronny Kinzer. It was an empty building. Whoever or whatever Ronny Kinzer was to Bike, he was invisible to everyone else.

By the time Miles reached his apartment that evening, he was frustrated. While in the shower, he mentally reviewed what facts he knew. All he could glean from the carousel of facts was that bullets from the same gun had killed Bike, the potential blackmailer, and Dexter, the potential purse snatcher. But hit men tended to use fairly common weapons. A suppressed .22 was deadly, but left few clues as to the identity of the killer.

~

Erin paced the floor of her bedroom, her parents having taken their coffee out to the front porch swing. The house was too quiet. She needed action. She had checked the locks at all possible entries. She paused at the window and peeked out at the patrol car parked in front of the house. Then she went to the kitchen for a glass of iced tea.

Bike was dead. Dexter was dead. She hadn't known either of them personally, had only stumbled into this mess accidentally. So, with them both dead, she should no longer be in danger.

No. The guy who had shot Dexter thought she could identify him.

The weekend had passed without incident, with a patrol car always near, even at church. And she had eaten a piece of cinnamon toast while her parents had bacon and eggs earlier that morning. But she needed interaction with someone besides her parents, someone who knew her well and exerted a calming influence over her.

She went to the living room, took her phone from her purse and dialed Ginger's cell number.

"Can you find tine to meet for lunch today?" she asked when her friend answered.

"I was just thinking of you as I dressed for work and was planning to call you. Should I meet you at your office?"

"That'll work."

After they agreed on a time and disconnected, Erin grabbed her purse and went out to meet Miles, whose truck had just pulled up behind the patrol car that was rolling into the street.

When she scooted into the passenger seat beside him, his tentative smile made her wonder if the closeness they had shared the last time they sat together in this vehicle had been a mirage.

It had been real for her, but she couldn't be sure if it had been for him.

"Ginger's meeting me for lunch." She said the first thing that popped into her mind.

Furrows creased his brow. "I hope you're not planning to leave the mall."

His concern touched her. "We'll eat on the premises."

He nodded and pulled into the street.

Shortly before noon, Erin finished with her last morning appointment and went to the front office just as Ginger stepped through the doorway.

"I'm craving tacos," she announced, giving Erin a hug.

Erin turned toward the counter where Lydia was making an appointment over the phone. "Lock up and put the sign on the door if you want to go out," she told her assistant. "I'll be back in time for my one-thirty appointment."

Lydia gave a thumbs-up and continued her conversation.

When Erin and Ginger reached the taco stand, they placed their orders and went to a corner table. Once they were seated, Erin noticed that Ginger didn't look so good. There were lines on her forehead and around her eyes, as if she had a headache.

"You okay?" she asked.

Ginger shrugged and didn't quite meet her eyes. "I'm fine."

"Are you sure?"

Ginger set her purse beside her. "Things have been extra busy at work lately. I'm just tired. How about you? I've been worried about you."

The arrival of their order saved her from having to respond. They each took their items from the tray and ate in silence for a few minutes. Then Ginger returned to her unanswered question.

"Are you okay? Bring me up to date on your situation."

She knew about the shootings. Everyone did.

Erin shared what she could. About her fears. And being under guard all the time. As she finished, Ginger's expression became sober. "Is there more between you and the security guard than you're admitting?"

Erin drew a deep sigh. "I'm not sure how to answer that."

"I get the impression there's more to him than meets the eye."

"There is, but I can't talk about it. There's nothing indecent between us, though."

Ginger reached over and placed her right hand over Erin's left one. "I never thought there was."

"I like him," Erin admitted. "Maybe too much. But I can't see anything coming of it."

Ginger grinned. "That's enough for now. But if you ever need a confidant, you know I'm available."

Erin turned her palm over and squeezed her friend's hand. "I know. Thanks."

Ginger smiled. Then a pensive look came over her face. "I've heard rumors about drugs floating through there. Do you think there's anything to them?"

Erin couldn't deny it. "Maybe."

A hint of understanding lit Ginger's expression. She took a big swallow of tea and set the cup down. "I hear rumors. There's a new guard. I won't ask any more. Where's the nearest restroom?"

Erin pointed. "It's right back there and to the left."

"Be right back." She scooped up her purse and hustled away.

When she returned minutes later, she wore an expression that Erin couldn't interpret. Anger? Worry? Concern?

Ginger scooted onto her chair and leaned forward. "I found a camera in the restroom."

Chapter 10

Miles didn't like the expressions on the faces of Erin and her friend. "What's wrong?" he asked as they approached him in the hallway.

Erin spoke. "Ginger found a camera in the bathroom at the taco food stand."

He managed to not roll his eyes in frustration. "I'll let the detective know that we need to do another mall-wide search. Thanks for the alert."

By the end of the day, he was pleased that no more cameras had been found in tanning salons or dressing rooms, but disgusted at a female officer's report of finding more in women's bathrooms. He had to wonder if Freddy the picture taker was responsible—but only fleetingly. Since the beating the young man had received, he didn't think so.

After work, he drove Erin to her Springfield home. "Patrol cars will be driving by here often," he said as he saw her to her door.

She thanked him and went inside, her solemn expression tearing at him. He didn't know how long this situation could remain static. Something had to give.

He woke more than once during the night, unable to reconcile his concern over Erin's safety with his common sense knowledge that she was being guarded closely. He felt responsible for her, yet understood her need to not stay with her parents all the time. She needed her independence and proximity to her business. But this lull couldn't. His gut knew that.

As he followed her to work the next morning, he was still delving for answers. They needed more information. The more he thought about it, the more convinced he became that he needed to talk to Archie Mullins again.

He checked his watch. He would escort Erin home after work, and then he would drive out to see the old man. Try to get more information from him.

He arrived at his usual post outside Erin's office a little early that afternoon and was surprised when she immediately exited.

"My last appointment was a no-show," she explained when she saw him. "So I figured I'd go ahead and leave so you don't have to wait around for me. Lydia will lock the door. I called the garage, and my car's not ready yet. The owner said they'll have it done tomorrow."

He escorted her to his truck and boosted her into the passenger seat. As he rounded the vehicle and climbed behind the wheel, he mentally reaffirmed his decision to not tell Erin where he was going, certain she would want to go with him.

He was just pulling out of the parking lot when a sound from behind the seat alerted him. Erin heard it too, he realized as their heads simultaneously swung to glance back over their shoulders. He had to focus forward again immediately as traffic filled every lane.

"Don't turn around," someone said. "And don't stop the truck. I just want to talk." The rough male voice came from the back floorboard.

"Who are you?" Miles demanded, keeping his eyes on the traffic around them.

"Archie Mullins. I can't be seen with you," the voice added in a rush.

"Do you have something to tell us?" Miles exchanged a sideways glance with Erin.

"Yeah. I figger you already know about the drugs. And I think them killins mean they're gettin' rid of people."

"Who's getting rid of people?"

"I don't know who's in charge."

"But you work for them," Miles said without taking his gaze off the road. This was a strange interview. He could tell that Erin was on full alert, should any kind of sudden action erupt.

"Yeah, but like I said, I don't know who the boss is."

"So how do you get your orders?"

The question was met with silence.

"Sooner or later you'll have to tell us." Miles spoke firmly.

"Okay, okay. Someone leaves packages with notes inside 'em at a certain spot in my daughter's place of business."

"You mean the antique booth at the flea market." He had to nail down the specifics.

It sounded like heavy breathing behind them. Then the old man finally spoke again. "Yeah. Then she passes 'em to whoever's name is on the sealed envelope inside the package."

"What else can you tell us?"

Another stretch of dead air. "I can show you a hideout in the hills where you can find …evidence."

Miles debated, but made a quick decision. He didn't like having Erin along, but the situation was immediate. On the other hand, he had her under his watchful eye. "Will you direct us there now?"

"If you want. Where are we now?"

Miles told him.

"Go south at the next exit."

From that point, he followed the old man's directions to a remote gravel road at the foot of a mountain and turned onto it. As they traveled upward, the forest deepened around them, the dense trees blocking the slightly lowering sun.

Miles glanced over at Erin. Though her face was shadowed, she sat erect in the seat, taking in details of their surroundings.

He also studied the terrain, wondering how high they would have to go, and whether they could be heading into a trap. He was debating whether to turn back when up ahead, through the trees, he recognized the dark outline of a building.

"I see a house," he said to the man behind them. "Do you think anyone's there?"

"I don't know." A note of fear sounded in the voice. "There's a place you can pull off the road several hundred yards before you get to it. You should see it any time." The old man suddenly sat up behind them and reached over the front seat to point. "There it is."

Miles pulled into the small clearing and took his binoculars from the glove compartment. He adjusted them and examined the hilltop. There were no vehicles visible in front of the house, but he could distinguish the bumpers of some around the far side and back.

He couldn't take any chances, though. He had to get his passengers out of here. As he started to remove the binoculars from his eyes, he paused. And peered closer at the patch of growth beyond the house. If he wasn't mistaken, they had just found a marijuana garden.

He shoved the binoculars back in the glove compartment, put the truck into a sharp U-turn and sped out of there.

~

Erin studied Miles's grim expression as he drove. She wanted to ask what he had seen, but didn't. She would ask after Archie was no longer behind them.

Miles drove back to the police station and parked in the lot. Then he turned to face Archie. "You're guilty of working for the drug operation. You can go in there and turn yourself in, or I can arrest you now. If you're honest with them, it could help your case."

Anger distorted the old man's face. His mouth twisted. "I helped you."

"That's right. They'll consider that. What you should consider is that you'll be safer in there until this matter is settled."

For a tense moment, Erin didn't think Archie would do as Miles said. But he looked at her, and then back at Miles, weighing the alternatives. His face twisted in a scowl. "All right, I'm going." He yanked the door open and climbed out.

Miles pulled out his phone and dialed a number. Erin listened as he told someone to look for Archie, and why. Within moments an officer appeared at the entrance of the police station and stepped out to meet Archie as he slowly made his way up the steps.

"That was good work," she said as Miles waved at the officer and put the truck in motion.

"I think the drug people have supplemented their meth and cocaine trade with a patch of marijuana," he said as he pulled into the street.

"That's what you saw with the binoculars?"

He nodded.

"What will you do now?"

"We need to raid that place, but I want to meet with Keaton and make some contacts first."

"If you need to go back to the mall, I have work I can do in my office until you're ready to leave."

"You're sure you don't mind?"

"I'm sure. I really need to clear up some paperwork."

"Okay." He pulled into the correct traffic lane and drove to the mall.

Once inside the building, he escorted her up the hall. "Lock the door as soon as you're in there," he instructed as she stepped inside the doorway. "Call me if you need anything."

She nodded. "I will. Take your time."

Over the next hour, Erin worked at her desk, catching up on correspondence and updating files. And suddenly realized how tired she was. She rubbed her eyes and flexed her tight shoulder and back muscles, thinking how nice it would be to sleep in tomorrow morning—and to be home in case she heard something of importance about the raid.

She was debating the matter when her phone rang. It was Miles. "Hello."

"Are you okay, or do you need to leave?"

"I'm fine. Are your plans coming together?"

"Yes, but we need to work out a couple more details. I'm in the storage room looking for something we need."

"How soon do you think the raid will go down?"

"In a few hours."

"You mean in the morning?"

"Uh huh. Gotta go."

Erin left her office and went to Lydia's desk. The appointment calendar her assistant kept within handy reach showed an unusually light schedule for the next day.

Erin took her phone from her pocket and dialed Lydia.

"What can I do for you?" Her assistant sounded surprised at an evening call.

"I'll not be coming to the office until after lunch tomorrow. I'd like you to reschedule my morning appointments as soon as you get here. You can call me if you need anything."

"Sure. Is there anything wrong?"

"No, I just need some time off, and I have an errand I need to run."

"Are you at the office now?"

"Yes. I returned to do some paperwork."

"I'll bet you were out with that hunky security guard who's been hanging around you so much, weren't you?"

Erin tamped down on a twinge of irritation. "I'm not going to answer that."

Lydia laughed. "Okay. See you after lunch tomorrow."

As Erin replaced her phone in her pocket, she glanced down at Lydia's desk calendar—and grinned at the collection of doodles around the edges of it. Her assistant was quite a cartoonist.

Not sure what she should do next, she considered her options, and decided she was too tired to think. Suddenly restless, she decided to walk down the hall and wait for Miles outside his office. He was the only person who knew she was here, and the complex was still busy with evening shoppers. There shouldn't be any safety risks.

She went back to her inner office, grabbed her purse and headed down the hallway. As she approached the flea market, the sight of a girl caught her attention. About five four, with long dark hair, Erin thought she resembled the girl in the surveillance footage.

She increased her pace, hoping for a better look, but the girl turned and disappeared amongst a cluster of people gathered around a clothing booth. By the time Erin reached the spot, the girl had disappeared.

~

Miles leaned back in the security office chair, facing Keaton across the desk. The local detective and a couple of deputies stood at the end of the desk facing the wall where the computer screen was angled so they could all see it. Together they had carefully mapped out how to execute the next morning's raid, including having a cop from the local department cover the mall duty in his absence.

"Does everyone understand his job?" Jed Parker, his superior, asked from the screen.

"Yeah," he and Keaton responded in unison. Others nodded.

"Then go get the bad guys." The screen went dark.

As Miles followed the others out of the office, he was surprised to find Erin leaning against the wall, waiting for him. "Got restless, huh?"

She pushed upright. "Yep."

Keaton grinned at them as he and the other officers headed back to their respective duties.

"I cancelled my morning appointments," Erin informed him as they headed to the exit. "I plan to sleep late."

"Good. I'll pass the word so whoever is parked outside your house will know. Should I tell them you want to pick up your car on your way to work?"

She smiled. "That would be great. Thanks."

"I'm starved," he said, stopping as they walked past a food stand. "I'd like to get some burgers to take home with me. Would you like some?"

Her stomach made a soft growl, and she felt heat rise in her face. "I would."

He laughed and tugged her to the counter beside him.

They ordered takeout and resumed their route to the parking lot.

They were both quiet on the drive to her house. "Stay inside," he instructed at her doorway, handing her one of the paper takeout bags.

"I'm going to eat, take a shower and go to bed. But I'll be praying for you in the morning. God will help you."

"Thanks. I needed that reminder."

The words encouraged him. Alongside them was the thought that he wanted to kiss her. He shouldn't. He knew that. But when she lifted her chin and their gazes locked, he leaned close, his heartbeat revving into overdrive. His lips grazed in a whisper over hers.

He backed away and placed a finger on her lower lip. "Good night."

The next morning, the team rode in silence to the gravel road that he had traveled up the hillside yesterday. As they rolled upward, Miles mentally rehearsed the approach they planned to take once they arrived. It was impossible to anticipate every possibility, but they had tried.

He pulled to a stop several hundred yards from the building where the trees and underbrush were thick enough to shield them from view. Binoculars in hand, he stepped to the ground, and the others circled around the open truck door.

He pointed at Keaton. "You circle around to the rear of the property. Radio me when you're set and wait for my signal."

"You want me to take that side?" One of the other officers pointed to the left.

Miles nodded.

While the team worked their way into place, he raised the binoculars to his eyes and moved the lenses over the area, breathing a silent prayer for everyone's safety. They all knew there was risk in such operations, but hoped for this one to go off without any injuries.

The house appeared empty. The place looked deserted. There was no sign of vehicles, even in the rear, no sign of activity anywhere.

"Can you see any movement?" he asked Keaton.

"Nope."

"Are you in place?" he asked the detective.

"Yep."

"All right. Proceed with caution."

Miles tossed the binoculars on the seat of his truck and grabbed the bullhorn. Then he eased the door shut and moved up the hill. He crossed the weed infested, unkempt yard and crouched behind a bush. At the corner of the house, Keaton had his back to the wall, his gun drawn and trained on the doorway.

Miles raised the bullhorn to his mouth. "This is the police. Come out of there with your hands in the air."

There was no response. Nothing moved.

Miles spoke into the horn again. "We have a warrant to search the premises. Come out with your hands raised."

He waited another full minute. Nothing happened.

He dropped the bullhorn onto the ground and raised a hand, signaling for the officers to cover him. Then he drew his gun and cautiously approached the doorway, alert for any motion or threat.

He was only a few feet away when the building erupted in a flaming blast. The impact sent him stumbling backward.

Chapter 11

Miles sat in a chair in the small security office, facing the police detective and two other officers. It was a tight fit, but they needed to finalize the report on their failed raid. He pressed an ice pack against his smarting jaw, thinking he could still taste the bitterness of ash on his lips. He flexed the jaw, testing the soreness of it and his stinging cheek.

"The fire destroyed the building and whatever evidence was in it," Keaton said. "Even the garden in the back that you told us about has been scraped off and hauled away. You had a close call. Someone knew we were coming and rigged the place to explode. But how did they know?"

Miles blew out a long breath of frustration. "I've been thinking about that. I'm afraid I have to take the blame."

All eyes focused on him. "How do you figure that?" the detective asked.

"Someone had to have seen my truck yesterday. I parked too close and failed to spot a lookout." He grimaced, his head pounding.

Keaton rubbed a hand over the bandage on his arm. "Maybe they were tipped off."

The detective frowned. "Who could have done that?"

Miles's heart thudded at realizing the only person who knew about the raid besides his partner and superior and these officers was Erin. But the idea was ludicrous that she would have said anything. She wouldn't even know who to tell if she had such an inclination.

Miles shook his head, wincing at the pain caused by the movement. "All I can say is we're up against some smart operators. They have money and resources, and I'm afraid they also have inside information. But we'll get them. We appreciate you working with us," he added, speaking to the deputies.

"You're helping us as well," one of them said. "Glad we can work as a team."

The session broke up, and they all returned to their respective duties.

~

"There's someone here to speak to you," Lydia said as Erin emerged from a treatment room into the hallway, an hour after having arrived at the office at one o'clock.

It was unusual for her assistant to contact her between patients this way. "Who is it?"

Lydia dipped her head, peering over the top of the narrow, oval reading frames she wore today. "It's your friend Freddy, and he said he's on his work break. He acts nervous."

"Okay, thanks. I'll see what he wants."

Erin went to the front office and found Freddy staring at the display rack of frames. He whipped around at her entrance. His gaze darted to the lady waiting for her appointment, to Lydia behind the counter, and then back to Erin. He swallowed. "I, uh, I saw that …"

"Let's go to my office," Erin interrupted, sensing he had come to tell her something relating to the case.

When he had followed her inside her office, Erin closed the door and faced him. "Now tell me what you saw."

"It was the girl you showed me in that security picture. I recognized her pretty hair—and the glittery shoes she was wearing."

Erin's mouth opened in pleasure. "Freddy, that's wonderful. What's her name?"

The smile that had been on his face turned to a look of consternation. "I don't know. I've just seen her around."

Her hopes sank. "You've never heard it?"

He started to shake his head, but paused. His expression turned pensive. The fingers of his right hand tapped against his thigh. "I saw her with another girl one day. And she called her …" His eyes squeezed shut. Then he opened them. "I think the other girl called her Shannon, or something like that. That's all I can remember."

"Thank you for coming and telling me this. If you remember anything else about her, or other things that might be going on around here that shouldn't be, will you please tell me?"

He beamed with pleasure. "I'll do that."

"The security people will also appreciate it when I tell them about this."

The smile faded at the reminder, but he nodded. "The guards were good to me."

"Maybe they'll find out who hurt you. Wouldn't you like that?"

His tousled head bobbed. "Yeah. They need to be arrested, so they can't hurt more people."

"Thanks again for coming, Freddy."

As soon as he was gone, Erin checked her watch. She had to take care of the lady waiting out front, but she had a few minutes between her and the next patient. She would call Miles then.

As soon as she had Mrs. Kelly taken care of, Erin went back to her office and called Miles. "Where are you?" she asked when he answered.

"Not far from your office. You need something?"

"Freddy just came to see me." She quickly related what he had told her.

"Thanks for letting me know. I'll see if I can figure out a last name to go with Shannon."

~

Miles completed his patrol round quickly and went to the security office. The sound of Erin's voice had stirred a longing in him, powerful in its intensity. It also stirred warnings. He had grown used to his solitary life. He had experienced love—and the heartache of losing the woman he loved. He couldn't consider risking that kind of painful cycle again.

And he had a job to do.

He seated himself in front of the surveillance camera and sat viewing footage of the flea market, lady dressing rooms and bathrooms, watching for anyone who resembled that young woman in height, body build and manner of walking, until his eyes burned.

Discouraged, he began viewing feed from another screen display. And jerked upright in the chair when he saw a young woman peer around in a furtive manner, then enter a dressing room, a garment draped over her arm. When she emerged in what he calculated too short a time to have changed into that garment and back into her own clothes, he had the distinct impression he had just witnessed the planting of a camera.

He shot from the chair and raced to that dressing room. But by the time he got there, the young woman was nowhere to be seen. Frustrated, he hurriedly located the camera he expected to find. Then he returned to the office and printed a copy of the girl's image. He took it, along with the one taken at the flea market next to where Erin's mistaken package incident had occurred and compared them. They matched. This picture showed her face, and he had a possible first name.

He set out on patrol again, seeking out business owners or managers and asking them if they recognized the girl and explaining that her first name might be Shannon. Some asked why he wanted to know and received a brief explanation about the cameras in the dressing rooms, with no mention of the drug case.

"I remember her," the manager at one of the fast food marts said when shown the pictures. "I don't remember her name, but it should be on the work application she filled out a few days ago. We didn't need anyone at the time, so I didn't interview her. Come with me." He beckoned.

Miles followed the man to a small office in the back of the business and waited while he took a stack of applications from a file cabinet and leafed through them. When he was more than halfway through the stack, he paused to study one more closely. Then he nodded in satisfaction. "I'm sure this is the one."

Miles took the application when it was offered. The name on it was Shannon Davis. "Can you make a copy of this for me?"

"I sure can." He did so and handed over the copy.

Miles thanked the guy and hurried back to the security office. Then he called Keaton.

"What's up?" his colleague asked.

Miles explained what he had learned. "I have a local address for her. Can you go check it, or would you rather relieve me here so I can do it?"

"I'll go look for her and get back to you."

Miles gave him the address, and they disconnected. Then he turned his attention back to the application. Under current employer, Miss Davis had listed Shepherd of the Hills Theater in Branson. It was another place to look for her, but it made him wonder why she was applying for another job. Maybe she was tired of commuting.

Suddenly another thought struck him. Bike's last name was Davis. Could they be related?

He did some computer research and discovered that Shannon was his sister. That meant her family was dealing with a funeral.

Other questions occurred. Was she involved in Bike's actions? If so, was she on the run?

The phone rang. It was Keaton. "Any luck?"

"No one was home at that address. I checked with the apartment manager, and he said she moved out over the weekend."

That strengthened his suspicion that she was hiding from someone. "Maybe she moved in with her family."

"Or a friend," Keaton suggested.

"But we can't know that. I wonder if she still works at the theater. Can you pick up a couple of tickets for the Shepherd of the Hills show and bring them to me when you come on duty?"

"Sure. But what does this have to do with finding this girl?"

He had forgotten that he hadn't told Keaton that. "I didn't think to tell you when I gave you that address, but she listed the theater as her place of employment."

"Ah, so you plan to attend the show to look for her— and take along a companion. May I guess whether that companion will be the pretty eye doctor?"

"Knock it off, pal. But, yeah, I was thinking along that line."

"Then I'll be happy to get the tickets for you, even though I'll probably have to pull some strings since it's tourist season. You're fortunate that this is a Thursday. They only do shows on Tuesdays, Thursdays and Saturdays."

As soon as they ended the call, Miles started to dial Erin. But he hesitated, thinking face to face persuasion might work better.

He strode down the hall to her office. When he stepped inside the doorway, the assistant smiled across the room at him. "I'll tell her you're here."

She went to the back and reappeared a minute later. "She said for you to go on into her office, and she'll meet you in about five minutes."

Miles went to the office and settled in a chair to wait. The orderliness of Erin's utilitarian workspace appealed to him.

"Did the name help?" Erin asked as she entered the room and closed the door.

"It did." He related his findings, including the girl's employment listing. "I asked Keaton to pick up two tickets for the outdoor drama, thinking you could attend with me. If you'd like," he added in a questioning inflection.

She smiled. "Of course I'd like. I want her found. And I want to help see that the drugs and killings are stopped. Have you ever seen the show?"

He shook his head. "I've heard about it, though. Do you know what time it starts?"

"Not until eight-thirty, if I remember correctly from when I took my parents last summer."

Perfect. "Rather than me following you home, why don't we leave your car here at the mall and go on to Branson right after work? We can have supper at the Shepherd's Mill Restaurant before the show." He grinned. "I've heard it's a nice place to eat."

"Shouldn't I go home and change clothes?"

He looked at her simple tan slacks and white kimono. "You're perfect as you are. I'll change out of my uniform, though. I keep some casual clothes in my truck. I'll be back for you at five."

He chuckled silently on his way to monitor the flea market. He hadn't been interested in dating since Shelly's death. But he had been experiencing some change, something approaching peace, this past week. Now here he was manufacturing ways to spend time with a woman. He still missed Shelly. He always would. But maybe it was time to move forward with his life.

His eyes burned. Life *was* moving on. The slow shifting from the past to the future hurt, but it was as it should be. Moving on meant letting go, though, and he didn't know if he could do that. He needed to proceed with caution.

When he met Erin at five o'clock, caution was not what he felt. Instead, the feelings inside him were deeper than he had thought.

"Tell me about the show," he said once they were traveling south on Highway 65 after leaving the mall.

"It's a passionate tale of the tough life of the mountain folk of Southern Missouri and Northern Arkansas in the late 1800s, as portrayed by Harold Bell Wright, a Christian minister, in his novel *The Shepherd of the Hills*," she quoted as if from long familiarity. "They utilize a cast of around ninety actors and actresses and over thirty animals."

They continued chatting while he drove to Branson and then took West 76 Country Boulevard to the Homestead. He parked in the lot, and they went to the nearby restaurant. The rustic décor of the spacious dining room featured barn wood walls with rusty tin ceilings and wood flooring. Windows surrounded the walls, with a large fireplace at one end of the room. A Model-T Ford automobile rested in a loft above a row of booths.

Miles ordered steak, and Erin had the Shepherd's Pie. He enjoyed every minute of their time together, lingering over cups of coffee at the end of the meal. Miles found himself reluctant to have it end, but realized he needed to focus on the purpose of the evening.

When the waitress placed a bill on the table, he faced her. "May I ask you a question?"

She paused. "Sure."

"We're looking for Shannon Davis. Do you know her?"

The middle-aged blond smiled. "She's a waitress here. She works the early shift, but she hasn't been in this week. Her brother's funeral was this morning." She paused. "Sometimes she comes back in the evenings to pick up her boyfriend after he gets all the show animals tended and back in their pens."

"Thank you. We'll watch for her."

He paid the bill, and they boarded a Jeep drawn tram that took them to the amphitheater.

Miles was impressed at the sight of an authentically detailed outdoor stage the size of a football field.

As they watched the live reenactment of Wright's novel, he kept an eye on the perimeter of the stage, paying particular attention to the animals and anyone near them.

When the drama ended, they remained seated while theater guests participated in a meet and greet time with the cast, seeking autographs and taking pictures.

Miles continued to focus on the animals being removed from the area, knowing that Erin was doing the same. Many were hidden by the shadows beyond the stage lights.

Suddenly she drew a sharp breath and leaned forward. "Is that her?"

Miles followed the line of her pointing finger to where a young woman stood next to a young man who held the reins of a horse. "I believe you're right."

Chapter 12

Erin watched Miles stride toward the couple at a fast speed, but not running, she assumed not wanting to cause alarm among the remaining cast and guests. He spoke into his phone as he proceeded.

Sensing she shouldn't interfere, she sat in self-imposed silence, her eyes glued to the scene playing out at the perimeter of the huge stage.

Miles approached the couple and spoke to them before focusing on the girl. The expression on her face turned angry at whatever he said to her. They spoke for another couple of minutes, and then the girl whirled and started to run away—but had her arm snagged by Miles. His face no longer held a pleasant expression, but one of sternness that bordered on fierce.

Movement in the aisle drew Erin's attention to her left. A police deputy strode at a near run toward the stage. By now people had begun to stare at what was happening.

Within minutes, the girl had been escorted from the premises by the officer, and Miles headed back toward Erin as she made her way to meet him.

"She's the girl we were looking for," he confirmed when they met. "She's being taken to local police headquarters. I need to meet them for her questioning."

"I don't mind waiting."

"If you're sure you don't mind, let's get to the station."

It was late when Miles emerged from the interrogation room into the front lobby of the police station where Erin sat. "She's definitely Harley's sister," he said on the drive back to Springfield and to the mall to get her car. "She's an addict, and she finally admitted to having bought drugs at the flea market. I showed her the picture proving she was there when someone set a package next to yours and you each took the wrong one, but she claims she has no idea who chased after you."

"Do you think she's lying about that?"

He changed traffic lanes. "I'm inclined to think she's not. As an addict, I think her focus was entirely on making her buy. I could be wrong, though. I think it's time to set up a sting. But I need to work out a plan with Keaton and the local police."

"What about the cameras? Did the girl admit planting those?"

"She did—after being fingerprinted and told that her prints will be compared to ones found on the camera—and that she was on video entering and exiting a dressing room. She did it for money to buy drugs."

Erin was impressed with the amount of information that had been obtained, but as they rode in silence, a huge question still bothered her. "Did she say who hired her?" she asked as they reached Springfield and headed toward the mall.

Miles shook his head, pulling into the mall parking lot. "She clammed up when asked that."

"Her brother's already dead. Do you think she's afraid of being killed?"

He drove up behind Erin's car and stopped. Putting the truck in neutral, he turned in the seat to face her. "I think she is. And she should be. Protecting the guy—assuming it's a guy—isn't going to keep her safe. The others were killed to keep them quiet. I'm afraid the same will happen to her."

Erin opened the door, but still faced the dome lit cab. "I wonder why she applied for a job at the mall."

His mouth pulled up at one side. "She may want to be closer to her drug source, or she may think she can juggle two jobs."

"Or both." Erin exited his truck, went to her car and headed home, Miles close behind her. When she arrived, a patrol car was just pulling to the curb. She waved goodbye at Miles and pulled into her driveway.

~

Miles spent Friday conducting constant surveillance—with the help of a couple of deputies—of the flea market vendors and their operators, trying to formulate a plan for nailing them. But by the end of the day not one buy had been detected. He had to face the reality that they didn't have enough information. And they couldn't risk questioning the woman too soon and alerting her.

In his gut he was convinced that more drugs had slipped past them. Frustration boiled.

When he met Erin after work, she was quiet until they had exited the building. "When does your sting go into operation?" she asked as they approached the employee parking lot.

"It doesn't."

Her head whipped around. "Why?"

"Not enough facts."

They reached her car, and she stood by the closed door, studying him in silence for several moments before speaking. "Then let's get more facts," she said bluntly.

He almost asked how, but paused. "We? You aren't responsible for doing that."

Hands went onto her hips. "But I want to be part of the investigation. I was made part of the case when I came under attack. These people have to be stopped. I need to help if I can."

He understood, but he couldn't put her at risk. Yet he found himself asking, "How do you propose getting more facts?"

"Is Shannon Davis still in jail?"

"Yes. But there's no proof on the drugs. She wasn't caught with them, or even witnessed with them. She's only being charged for placing the cameras."

"I'd like to talk to her. She has to know more than she's told," she rushed on, as if reading his expression. "I don't like taking advantage of her when she's just buried her brother, but that vulnerability, plus talking to a woman, could make her more forthcoming."

He considered for several moments, torn, but coming to the reluctant conclusion that she was right. "Okay," he finally agreed. "Get in my truck, and I'll take you to the police station."

When they entered the building minutes later, Miles spoke to the officer at the front desk, and they were shown to a small room furnished with a rectangular table and four chairs. They took seats facing one another near one end of the table.

After a five minute wait, a stony faced Shannon Davis was escorted into the room and to the chair at the end of the table between them. She wore the same jeans and tank top as last night. Her long dark hair was mussed, her eyes red rimmed. She looked older than the nineteen or twenty Miles estimated her to be.

He settled back to watch and listen.

~

"I'm truly sorry about your brother," Erin said, aching for the girl. "I know you're going through a tough time, but surely you want to see your brother's killer brought to justice, don't you? Your help is needed to do that."

Shannon remained silent, but clenched her hands together in her lap to still the trembling visible in her fingers. Fear radiated from her swollen eyes.

Erin leaned forward. "You're afraid. I understand that. You have reason to be. The only way to be safe is to stop the killing. Protecting the guy who supplies the drugs sold at the mall, and who is probably the person who hired you, isn't going to keep you safe. Others have been killed to keep them quiet. Please don't let that happen to you. Help us stop him."

Her mouth trembling, Shannon blinked back tears. "Okay," she said so softly Erin could hardly hear her. Then she covered her face with her hands, choking on sobs.

Erin waited a few moments for Shannon to regain her composure. Once the girl had calmed a bit, she asked, "How are the drugs sold without being detected?"

Shannon removed her hands from her face and wiped them over her eyes. "You have to know how to ask," she said hoarsely.

"How is that?"

She swiped at her eyes again. "You have to say you want merchandise from the van," she blurted in a rush.

Erin nodded, elated at hearing how they did it. The drugs weren't detected because they were never brought inside. The contact was all that was done inside. "And do you have to know which vendor to contact on certain days?"

Shannon nodded in short, jerky motions.

"The day you were filmed at the antique booth was a Wednesday."

Another nod.

"Do you remember who had already made a buy and was near you that day?"

What looked like genuine puzzlement came over the girl's face. She thought for a moment, frowning, and then shook her head. "I don't know."

Hoping to prod the girl's memory, Erin reached over and placed a hand over one of Shannon's. "There was a mix-up that day. I bought something at the next booth and set it down for a few moments. After I picked up what I thought was my package and left, someone ran me off the highway and took the package from my car. When I returned later and asked the vendor about my package, she had saved it for me. She said she found it on the floor."

The crease lines in Shannon's brow deepened. "That's strange."

"The only thing I can figure is that someone had made a buy, returned to talk to the vendor and set his or her package beside mine. Then, either I took the wrong one, or he or she mistakenly took mine and I picked up what was left. When he discovered the mix-up, he ran me down to get it back."

The girl's head continued to move slowly back and forth. "I don't know who it would have been. Lots of people go through there." She paused, as if struck by a new thought. "Old Nag might know."

Erin exchanged a fleeting glance with Miles, and then looked Shannon directly in the eye. "Your brother called the lady who sells antiques that, didn't he?"

The reminder of her brother brought fresh tears flowing. Shannon's head bobbed jerkily. "He had a nickname, so he thought others should have them, too."

Miles reached over and rubbed her other hand. "Thank you, Shannon. You've been a big help. But I have one more question. Was it Leland Zink who hired you to plant those cameras?"

Shannon's eyes rounded in fear. "I don't know. I guess it could have been." She inhaled a deep breath. "I got a phone call offering me money and saying it would be left in my car after I did what was instructed. I left the car unlocked like he said, and the money was there when I returned."

Erin nodded in understanding. "Then it happened again."

"Yes."

After they thanked her again, Erin's thoughts kept her silent as they left the police station.

"So Leland is still most likely the boss," Miles said once they were inside his truck, staring forward. "He's running drugs through the flea market and a porn operation in the entire mall."

Erin fastened her seat belt while he started the engine and turned the air conditioning on high, summoning courage to voice her idea. "He can't be stopped too soon. I could try to make a buy for you."

He faced her, brows drawn together in a glower. "No."

Her shoulders shot up a notch. "Yes. Cops—or agents—are too recognizable."

"People around the mall know you," he snapped back.

"I'll wear a disguise."

A finger tapped over his upper lip, a slight twitch forming at the corners of his mouth as his gaze traveled over her. "You'd be hard to disguise."

She suppressed a sudden urge to laugh. "I can do it. And I'd be a good customer. You need proof that Leland is behind everything, and I can help you get it. I want to do it. You need to shut down that operation before more people end up dead."

Miles put the truck in motion. He didn't speak again until he pulled up beside her car in the mall parking lot. Then he faced her, the motor and air still running. "It's against my better judgment, but I'll talk to my superior and Keaton. But if they like the idea and approve it, you have to promise you'll be careful."

"Of course I will. And while you're making your contacts, I'll put together a good disguise."

He grinned, his manner less tense. "I can't wait to see it."

"Tomorrow is Saturday, so it's perfect since I won't be working at my clinic." Another thought struck. "And the S next to Worm on Bike's list means I should try to buy at the book seller booths. I think there are three of them in the market."

"After I follow you home, I'll come back to the office to talk to Keaton and call my superior. I'll let you know if it's a go."

Satisfied, Erin went to her car, drove home and waved at Miles as he backed out of her drive and headed back to the mall.

He called her two hours later and said there would be officers stationed out of sight in the mall the next morning, ready to move in at a moment's notice. She was to wear a wire and say 'Done' the second she made a buy and had the goods.

When she climbed into his truck and placed her overnight bag at her feet the next morning, he practically gaped at her.

"Who is this stranger in my truck?" he asked after a laugh. "The outfit's great, but why are you limping?"

"I'm wearing a knee brace to give me a natural limp." She wore a blond wig that she had tweaked to give it dark roots, wrap-around sunglasses, and thick-soled sandals with wide leather straps. Her knee-length shorts were baggy and paired with a baseball jersey over a waist and thighs padded with towels to make her appear heavier. A fanny pack was belted around her waist and rested on her hip.

"This is too serious for laughing," he said on the way to the mall. "But it's the funniest sight I've seen in ages."

"Is Keaton in the office?" she asked, glad he could find amusement in anything about this situation.

Miles pulled into the parking lot. "He's expecting you. I'll follow you inside to be sure no one sees you go into the security office, and that everyone's in place. As soon as you're wired, wander around a bit, and then approach those book booths. If you make a buy, say 'Done' and we'll arrest the seller. Okay?"

She nodded. "Got it." She exited the truck and headed inside, mindful of Miles behind her.

~

Miles kept his eye on the limping figure ahead of him, too on edge to find any more humor in this. Erin's determination and courage impressed him. But he had to keep his mind on business. Right now she was a colleague. Nothing more, he reminded himself.

When she emerged from the security office only a few minutes after entering, he made eye contact from down the hall. When she nodded that she was wired, he moved to a position around the corner from the flea market. He was in uniform, so sight of him shouldn't raise any questions, no matter where he was stationed, but he kept his distance.

He walked the hallway, listening to sounds coming from Erin's wire. His gut clenched when she approached a book vendor and said she wanted merchandise from the van.

There was silence for several seconds. Peeking around the corner, he watched the vendor, an older man, studying her in intense scrutiny.

"We don't have any merchandise in no van, Ma'am. You must be mistaken."

The vendor's words brought frustration—but relief that Erin wasn't in danger.

Miles listened through two more attempts, with similar results. When she met him near the security office, he read disappointment in her expression and body language.

"I want to try again," she informed him when he had followed her back to his truck.

He didn't want her in danger, but she seemed their best shot at this point. And she was set on it. "I'll talk it over with the team and let you know tomorrow."

That seemed to placate her.

"I know you have to go to work," she said after he drove to Ozark and parked in front of her parents' house where she would spend the weekend.

Miles wasn't sure how she would explain her appearance, but he knew the parents were trustworthy.

"Mom gave me orders to invite you to lunch with us after church tomorrow," she said. "Are you going?"

"I'll meet you there."

"You don't need to see me to the door." She climbed out, carrying her bag and limping to meet her mother on the porch. She turned and waved as he pulled away from the curb.

Back at the mall, his team decided they did want to try again.

The next day, he joined the Stuart family at church—and found the service uplifting. Members of the congregation chatted with him and made him feel welcome. It was all good.

Lunch with Erin's parents was also good. Afterward, she took his hand and led him to the living room. "What's the verdict?" she wasted no time asking.

"We'll give it another try. Tomorrow after work, I'll follow you home as usual. Then you can change into your disguise, and we'll go back to try again." She would stay in Springfield during the week.

She smiled warmly. "It's a good plan. I'm glad you came to church and ate lunch with us today. Are you glad you came?"

"It was nice."

"Good. I guess I'll see you tomorrow."

He left with a spring in his step—and trepidation in his gut.

Chapter 13

Erin limped from one flea market booth to another, working her way toward the one selling baby clothes. This was Monday afternoon, and Bike's list had an M beside Wee Duds.

She wore the disguise she had used Saturday, having gone home after work, changed and returned so she would have been observed leaving as usual in case anyone was watching.

A quiet, "Ma'am," from the book vendor she was moving past took her by surprise. It was the first vendor she had approached Saturday. He beckoned for her to come nearer.

She limped to a halt in front of him. "Are you talking to me?" she asked, wanting to be sure Miles and Keaton heard this, whatever it was.

The sixtyish man nodded, his eyes darting around as if assuring privacy. When he leaned forward over his table, she bent toward him, putting the microphone concealed under her jersey within closer range of his voice.

"We have new supplies in stock, if you're still interested."

"Where?" she asked quietly, nodding.

"In the white van at the north corner of the parking lot," he said in a raspy voice. "Say Woody sent you."

Erin nodded and headed for the exit. She waited until she was outside the doorway to speak. "You got that?"

"Got it," Miles responded. "We're moving to the exits. Have you spotted the van yet?"

Scanning the area, her gaze halted on an older white van in the section of the lot to her right. "I just spotted it, and I'm headed that way." She walked that direction as she spoke, making as little mouth movement as possible.

"We're ready. Be careful."

Her heart thudded as she approached the vehicle, unable to distinguish anyone behind the dark tinted glass. But as she reached the side of it, the driver's window lowered. A woman she recognized from the baby clothes booth stared out at her.

"Woody sent me," Erin said quietly, darting a furtive glance around them, as if afraid of being detected.

The woman studied her in cold assessment. Then she opened the door. "How much do you need?"

"Two grams is all I can afford today."

The woman reached over and extracted a small bag from a container in the floorboard near her feet. "You know the price," she said, holding onto the package, clearly not about to release the goods until she had been paid.

Erin pulled the fanny pack around in front of her and took out the amount Miles said Shannon had quoted. The woman took the bills and counted them before handing over the bag of cocaine. Then the window went up.

"Done," Erin said as she stepped away from the van. Immediately she spied armed officers spilling from the building. Miles had apparently gotten a head start and worked his way through the parking lot, because he suddenly appeared from around the side of the van. He made an emphatic hand motion for Erin to scram.

"Open the door. You're under arrest," he yelled as she ran across the lot.

~

The tightness in his chest eased when Miles saw that Erin had made it out of the line of possible gunfire. He jerked the van door open and held his gun steady as the woman stepped to the pavement and was cuffed by Keaton. Her eyes and red face radiated sheer rage.

Woody, the guy from the book booth who had sent Erin out here, had already been arrested by one of the local deputies. Woody might just be questioned and released, since he hadn't been caught with the goods. But this woman had goods in her possession. Both were put in a patrol car and taken to the police station.

"I'll go back on mall duty if you want to oversee the interrogations," Keaton offered as the patrol car drove away.

"Thanks." Miles headed for his truck, where Erin had hidden in the back seat as planned. He circled around and dropped her at her house. He didn't like her staying there alone, but with people behind bars and patrol cars still guarding her, she insisted she was safe. When she slipped a key into her door lock, he wished he had a reason to stick around, but he had to get to the police station, leaving him no choice but to leave.

As anticipated, the woman, whose name was Wendy Dawson, was formally charged and jailed. Woodrow Young was being held overnight, a bail hearing scheduled for the next morning.

That was good—but unsatisfactory. According to Bike's list, two more booth operators were dealing drugs. And there could be more. The antiques dealer would be taken in for questioning, but would be released for lack of evidence, since she wasn't implicated in this particular drug sale. Ringer, the mobile phone dealer who had fled, had never returned to his booth. It was still there, but run by a different person. Mark Hammond's continued absence bugged Miles.

Yes, arrests had been made. They had the satisfaction of having taken a bunch of drugs out of circulation. But it wasn't enough. They needed to nail the whole outfit—and the kingpin. They needed to find out who was behind the organization. He hoped information could be extracted from those who had been arrested.

Miles returned to the security office and booted the computer. Over the next two hours he searched and learned more about each of the vendors in that market, paying particular attention to the ones on Bike's list. Wendy Dawson, the woman they had arrested earlier that afternoon, had a history of alcohol abuse, to the point that her children had been placed in foster care.

Mark Hammond, the absent mobile phone vendor, had been arrested in a bar fight a few weeks earlier, but that was the only blot on his record. But he had run. He was involved in the drug operation. Miles had no doubt of that.

His eyes bleary from reading at the computer screen, Miles leaned back and rubbed them. What was eluding him?

He was tired. Make that exhausted. His brain had short circuited. He shut down the computer and went to his apartment.

Tuesday morning he woke early, downed a quick donut and glass of milk, and then drove back to police headquarters before work hours at the mall.

"I'd like to talk to Wendy Dawson again," he said to the deputy on duty.

"I'll get her." He took keys from the peg board behind him. "I assume you want her in the interrogation room."

"Yes. I have a few more questions for her." He made his way to the room and took a seat.

When the woman was brought in and seated across the table from him, Miles leaned forward so he was eye level with her. "Listen to me carefully, Wendy," he said in a tone meant to intimidate. "I'm going to make this offer only once. If you give me the name of the person running the drug operation, I'll speak to the judge and tell him you cooperated."

The scrawny woman glared at him, arms crossed over her chest. "I tell you that, I'm dead. Go away."

"You walk out that door," he said, pointing toward the front of the building, "without telling us, you'll probably be just as dead."

Her face went parchment pale, but she remained silent.

He splayed his hands on the tabletop, wishing he could siphon the information from her. "Okay, let's try this. I'll say a name, and you say yes or no. Will you do that much? It's in your best interest," he added forcefully. "Is it Leland Zink?"

The woman swallowed, her eyes drilling him.

"Yes," she finally whispered.

Miles pushed to his feet. "Thank you."

He tapped on the door and told the deputy who appeared that she could be taken back to her cell. Then he went to the detective's office and explained that he would be arresting Leland Zink as soon as possible.

"Call if you need anything," the chief said as Miles left the room.

As he walked to his truck, Miles pulled out his phone and called to update his superior. Then he called Keaton. "We have an arrest to make. Can you meet me at the mall?"

"For that I can be out of bed and dressed in a flash. Who are we arresting?"

"Yesterday's arrestee just confirmed that Leland is the boss. I'll swing around by Erin's and escort her to work while you do that."

Minutes later, he pulled to the curb behind the patrol car posted outside Erin's house and called her. "You ready?"

The door opened. "I am." Grinning, she disconnected and locked the door.

He followed her to the mall and parked next to her car. As he accompanied her to the entrance, he wanted to tell her what was stirring, but didn't think he should. She didn't need the stress, and it would be more satisfying to tell her after the arrest was made. But she needed a warning, he decided in an abrupt change of mind.

"Don't be alarmed if you hear a disturbance from the flea market this morning," he told her before entering the complex.

She paused at the entrance and faced him. "Are you making another arrest?"

"That's the intent. Go on about your work, and I'll contact you later."

She studied him, questions in her expression, but then seemed to accept the way of things. "I'll be on alert."

Miles saw her to her office and headed to the security office. The surveillance feed showed no sign of Leland on the premises, but he saw Keaton inside the front entrance, scanning the area. Everything appeared peaceful in the flea market area.

He dialed Keaton. "No sign of him on surveillance footage. See if you can find his car in the lot. He drives a dark colored SUV."

"I know the one. I'll check." Keaton turned and went back the way he had come.

Miles watched on the screen as Keaton rounded the building and strode through the lot, searching. He disappeared from camera range a couple of times, but soon reappeared.

Miles didn't have a wealth of patience. And this was making him edgy. Suddenly the screen showed a vehicle rolling into the lot. "He's pulling in at the south entrance," he informed Keaton while moving to the door. "I'm on my way."

He raced out of the building and looped around to the section of the parking lot where he had seen the SUV. He and Keaton reached the vehicle, one on either side, as the flea market owner stepped to the pavement.

Leland halted, his gaze darting from one to the other of them, his muscles visibly tightening. "What's with you two?"

"You're under arrest, Leland."

"You're crazy." Although he sounded adamant, Miles detected a note of panic in his voice.

While Miles held his gun on Leland, Keaton moved around the SUV and frisked him.

"Hey!" Leland twisted, bucking against him when Keaton latched onto his arm.

"Don't make me use this," Miles warned, stepping closer, his gun raised.

Leland went motionless, but when Keaton started to cuff him, he stiffened and bucked against the hold. A fist swung upward and slammed Keaton in the jaw.

"Don't move," Miles barked, his lethal tone making the man freeze. "Keep your hands where I can see them."

Leland stared at them, a feverish gleam in his eyes. "I want a lawyer."

"I'll read him his rights and haul him to jail," Keaton said, marching the man to his cruiser, citing as they went. Miles followed to make sure he was secure before leaving.

As they drove away, Miles returned to the mall to make some contacts.

He texted Erin to let her know the arrest had been made outside the building, not wanting her to worry if she was waiting for the sounds of a disturbance and not hearing it.

She texted back.

Good. Should be safe now and no longer need a bodyguard.

He texted again.

We'll talk about it after work.

After reporting to his supervisor, he contacted mall headquarters and let them know that their regular guards could return to their positions. He had details to clear up, but his undercover role had been exposed. He would finish the case under his own identity.

That done, he dealt with paperwork regarding the case. As he worked, he received a call saying that the guard whose place Keaton had taken would be back tomorrow, but that the one Miles had replaced couldn't be there until the next day. When asked if he could cover it one more day, Miles agreed, finding that he welcomed the reprieve.

Closing the case would mean it was time for him to return to St. Louis. The thought brought a wrench. He had to go. He didn't want to leave here. He was torn.

Chapter 14

"**Are you sure** this is necessary?" Erin asked as Miles escorted her to her door after following her home. "The dealers are shut down. I'm safe. A bodyguard is no longer needed."

He frowned. "Mark Hammond is still on the loose. So is your purse snatcher's assassin, who thinks you can identify him. And they both think you saw what's on that flash drive."

She thought about all that. "Does that mean they think there's more information on it than what we've seen?"

"I think that's very possible. Your regular security guard is returning to duty Thursday, so tomorrow will be my last day in that role."

"Does that mean you're off the case?"

He shook his head. "It means I can move around more openly now, function as myself. And I'm not willing to take chances with your life, so I'm sticking close to you until I'm certain you don't need security."

Her heart thrummed at what sounded like more than merely concern coming from him—and the depth of her emotions toward him. They began leaning toward one another. Then she backed away, her breath uneven as she came to her senses. "I'm going to throw together a BLT. Would you care for one?"

His head tipped, studying the flush she knew had to be coloring her cheeks. "I am a bit hungry."

She unlocked the door and led him inside. "Make yourself comfortable," she said over her shoulder as she dropped her purse on the coffee table and went to the kitchen.

Sensing Miles following her, she wasn't surprised when he stepped to the counter beside her. "What can I do to help?" he asked.

"I guess you could make some toast while I cook the bacon. Bread is in there." She pointed at the bread box.

Erin found herself relaxing as they worked together, and then shared the simple fare of sandwiches, chips and iced tea.

"I have ice cream sandwiches in the freezer," she said when they finished. Then she laughed. "I just offered you a sandwich to top off a sandwich. How ..."

"Appropriate," he said before she could find an adjective. His chuckle vibrated through her. "You talked me into it. I'll have one."

She went and got two. "Mom said she and Dad plan to stop by the mall in the morning on their way home from a church meeting." She handed one of the ice cream sandwiches to Miles. "Their mission organizations collect used eyeglasses, and they have a box of them they want to add to the ones I have stored there."

His interest sharpened. "You said missions. How do you use such items?"

She resumed her seat. "They're cleaned and sent to some of the poorest countries in the world. Ministry teams dispense them through short-term missions. While doing free checkups and treatments and fitting recipients for their glasses, those people have the opportunity to hear the gospel message."

He eyed her in assessment. "By chance are you a member of a mission team?"

She smiled. "I am. In fact, I'm scheduled to go to Jamaica in early September." Sitting here with him was comfortable in a way she had never experienced with any man. She loved the deep timbre of his voice. And his physical attractiveness gave her stomach flutters.

"Have your parents spent their entire lives in ministry?"

"A good part of them. Dad surrendered to the ministry when he was twenty, and Mom married him when she was twenty and he was twenty-three. But I wasn't born until Mom was thirty-nine."

"So that makes you about …" his gaze ran over her in speculation, "your early thirties?"

She nodded. "I'm thirty-two, well past the youthful expectations of marriage and all that goes with it."

He grinned. "You don't look past anything to me. You're vibrant and would be a wonderful companion to any man, and mother to his children."

She swallowed her bite of ice cream, shaking her head. "My parents are in their seventies now and need me to look after them. And I couldn't saddle anyone with my school debt," she added with a touch of solemnity.

He downed a bite, one hand making a wave of dismissal. "You're paying it, aren't you?"

"Of course."

"You'd pay it no matter your circumstances, wouldn't you?"

"Sure."

"Then what's the big deal? Any man who loved you would know you weren't marrying him for his money, and he would want to see your debt paid, would want to help eliminate it."

She shoved another bite into her mouth, momentarily without a response. So she swallowed and went on the offense. "What about you? You're still young, a man any woman would be proud to have as a husband. I'm sorry," she said, seeing the look of pain that flashed across his face. "I know you loved your wife, and that you still do."

His gaze trapped her. "I won't deny that it's been tough, but I think I'm on the brink of letting go of the past."

"I could understand why you wouldn't be willing to do that," she said, meaning it. It had to be terribly difficult to risk losing another person he loved, having already known a life with someone that had only lasted such a short time. She blinked back tears that threatened. "To let go and grasp someone new would seem like betrayal, wouldn't it?"

He nodded, his ice cream momentarily forgotten. "It has seemed that way, but lately I've been feeling that maybe it's time to move past that feeling. Shelly was a wonderful, loving person, and I'm sure she'd want me to be happy. I'm making progress."

"Do you have siblings?" she asked, needing to change the subject.

"I have an older sister who lives in Hot Springs. She and her husband both teach school. They have two boys who are seven and nine, and a five-year-old girl."

She grinned. "And I bet the girl rules the roost."

He chuckled. "You'd be right."

Erin stood and tossed her wrapper in the trash, along with the last bite of ice cream that she couldn't eat right now. "What will you do when this case is closed?" she asked, needing to divert the topic.

He also stood, his wrapper following hers into the trash. "I'll return to St. Louis for hopefully a little break and then a new assignment."

He stepped next to her and cupped her cheek. "I never thought I'd feel the way I do about anyone again. I admire you and find that I never get tired of spending time with you."

She smiled. "I'm not going anywhere."

~

Miles stood at a vantage point that offered a good view of the mall entrance. He watched people in summer garb swarm the hallways, the entrance and exit doors sliding open and closed in synchronized rhythm, while his mind ran on multiple tracks.

Of the list in Bike's flash drive, Nag, Worm, and Wee Duds had all been taken out of action. But Ringer couldn't be found. Would he, like Bike and Dexter, turn up dead? What was his relationship to Leland? Questions haunted Miles.

Was the operation shut down, or had someone else taken up the reins?

He couldn't do much about it today, but Keaton was already free of the evening security guard duties. Hopefully he was having some luck tracking the missing criminals.

A flurry of activity at the entrance claimed his attention. A uniformed male strode through the automatic door. Then Senator Fielder appeared, followed by two men in dark suits.

At the politician's appearance, people stopped to watch him or approach and shake his hand, while others smiled and went on about their business.

Fielder wasn't the only politician who had made an appearance this morning, seizing an opportunity for campaigning after word of the arrests at the mall had hit the news.

Erin's parents came through the entrance next, Verna's hand on Everett's arm. They stopped and spoke to the senator and shook his hand before heading on toward Erin's office. Everett carried a box that Miles assumed held the used eyeglasses Erin had told him about.

Everett smiled at Miles as they approached.

"Hello, Miles," Verna greeted him as he shook hands with her. Then she stepped closer and spoke softly. "Your cologne is memorable."

Miles chuckled at realizing how she had recognized him. "I'll stick to the brand so you'll always know when I'm around."

She patted his arm. "You do that."

When they had continued on their way, Miles looked back at where the politician stood speaking to people, smiling in practiced friendliness. Fielder's voice carried clearly. "I'm concerned about the crime in our area, but it's good to see business being done here as usual."

"It's good to see you visiting our businesses," someone responded. "Thank you for checking on them."

Miles scanned the crowd of shoppers and business people as the congressman continued to chat with people. Some were supporters, others potential supporters—the quest of any politician.

As the crowd circulated, chatting and debating, his phone rang. One of the businesses had caught a shoplifter. He headed that way.

While having lunch later in the security office, Miles watched surveillance footage of the mall. When he finished his burger, he leaned his head back against the chair. Still watching the flow of movement in the retail complex, he again had the nagging feeling that he was missing something. Some question hadn't been answered. But what was it?

Suddenly it hit him. Who had run Erin off the road to recover that package?

They had recovered some prints from the passenger door handle of her car after the incident, but hadn't been able to match them to anyone in the system.

As he dwelt on it, his thoughts shifted to Mark Hammond's absence. He needed to see if he could find a set of that guy's prints. He took the print kit from its storage place and went to the mobile phone booth where the guy who currently ran it had already left for the day. Tarps had been draped over the table.

Miles removed the tarp and eyed the place where Hammond's and his replacement's prints would be isolated from the shoppers who passed through the area. He concentrated on the area where he recalled seeing Mark pull a cash box from concealment under a pile of items near the table leg next to his chair. When he had lifted several prints, he returned to the office and went to work, processing prints and checking them against the database.

He had multiples of only two sets, so he concentrated on those—and found a match for one of them.

Slowly he revised his theory about the package mix-up. He pictured Hammond talking business with the antiques vendor and setting a package on the end of the table for a moment while doing something, maybe reaching into his pocket. Then, distracted, he picked up Erin's package by mistake, leaving his to be taken by her. When he discovered the error, he had panicked and gone racing after her—and would probably have killed her if there had been time. The thought sent a shiver through Miles.

He headed back to the flea market, feeling he was running in circles. This time he approached Harriet Wickham at her antiques booth, in no mood to mince words. If looks could kill, he would have been a corpse as the woman looked up and realized she was his objective.

"What are you doing back here?" she snapped, her mouth twisting into a snarl.

Miles didn't let her hostility faze him. "I think you know. I want an answer. When Doctor Stuart ended up with the wrong package, she thought it was her fault. But it wasn't, was it?"

She glared. "I don't know what you're talking about."

"I think you do. Someone was having a business discussion with you, and he was carrying a package. For some reason he set it down next to the one Doctor Stuart had just placed there and reached into his pocket for something, not noticing there was already another package sitting there.

It was probably only there a moment, but when he picked it up, still talking to you, he took the wrong one. And she took his, thinking it was hers.”

The woman continued to glare as he spoke, her head moving back and forth.

“When he noticed the error, or maybe you’re the one who noticed and pointed it out to him, he ran after the doctor. When he saw she was already in her car, he jumped into his and followed her, ran her off the road and recovered his package. Tell me who you were talking to that Wednesday.”

Her mouth tightened, her arms crossing in front of her.

Miles leaned down, hands flat on the table, and stared into her eyes. “Talk to me.”

She made a derisive snort. “My dad talked to you, and you took him to jail.”

“And you’re going to end up there talking to the local cops. Which will it be, me or them? Tell me who was at your table that day—and why.”

“Get lost.”

“It was Mark Hammond, wasn’t it? And you were talking business with him, probably drug business. You’ve been seen on surveillance handing him notes. Admit it, or I’m calling the police detective, an acquaintance of yours.” He pulled out his phone and poised a finger over it.

She remained quiet for so long he almost accepted defeat. But then, at last, she said, “It was him. You got it right.”

“Thanks. You’ve done the right thing.”

He was on his way back to the office, his thoughts tumbling, when his phone rang. It was Keaton. “Yeah.”

“Leland just made bail.”

Chapter 15

"You have a corneal abrasion from rubbing too hard when you got dirt in your eye. I'll give you some eye drops to prevent infection." Erin stepped away from the exam chair where her mother sat. "Sit tight and I'll write the prescription."

Verna eased forward in the chair. "We saw your friend Miles near the entrance when we arrived. How close are the two of you?"

Erin exhaled slowly and returned to her mother's side. "I like him. We're friends." She handed over the prescription.

Her mother reached over and placed a hand on Erin's arm. "I don't want to pry, but if there's anything you'd like to share, I'm listening."

Emitting a sigh, Erin placed a hand over her mother's. "I don't know if I'm ready to do that yet. But I admit I like him a lot."

Verna nodded. "Have you learned much about him?"

"Some. He was married to his high school sweetheart, but only for a short time. She died from a serious heart condition."

"And he married her, knowing she had it?"

Erin nodded, even though her mother couldn't see the gesture. "He loved her very much. And I'm sure he misses her terribly. He's learned to be strong, but he's not looking for more than friendship from another woman."

Verna raised her face. "Will you promise me one thing?"

Erin patted the hand beneath hers. "If it doesn't involve anything that will land me in jail."

Her mother smiled at the jest, then returned to serious mode. "Please don't think you need to stay single and take care of Dad and me. We love you and are proud of you, but we don't want you to devote your entire life to taking care of us. If you find someone to love, marry him and have a family. God will take care of us all."

Erin swallowed at the genuine love she knew prompted the little speech. She couldn't find words to respond.

"We'll be praying for you—and that young man," Verna continued. "I hope you'll do the same."

She could respond to that. "I will. Thanks, Mom." She placed a kiss on Verna's cheek.

Verna pushed to her feet and replaced her hand on Erin's arm for guidance back to the office where Everett waited.

"The church has collected almost enough money for the team's mission trip," her dad announced as they entered the room.

"Good. I've been preparing a bag of supplies." The amount of baggage they could take on the plane was limited, so Erin packed a bag of the most essential items she would need. After having made three previous mission trips, she had a good idea what to take. "I'll clean those glasses you brought and add them to the supply we plan to ship ahead of us."

After they were gone, Erin went to her next patient. When she finished with that one, she cleaned the glasses and took them to Lydia. "Add these to the ones in storage when you have time. I'd appreciate it if you would get the entire batch ready for shipping. I'll give you the address."

Lydia frowned and removed her round eyeglasses. She pressed her fingers to her temples, wincing. "Does it have to be done today? I have a pounding headache and was getting ready to ask if I could go home."

"It can wait. Go on home and get some rest. Call me this evening and let me know how you're feeling. Okay?"

Lydia nodded. "Thanks."

When her assistant was gone, Erin sighed in frustration. She had an important business related errand she had meant to ask Lydia to run. Now, not only did she have to do that, but she had to take care of the office duties as well as her patients.

She drew a deep breath and greeted the patient entering the room.

By the end of the day, Erin was bushed. When she left the office, Miles was waiting in his usual spot by the door. It was to be his final day. The thought hit her like a thunderbolt.

He moved over beside her as she locked the door. "I'll still see you to and from work until the case is closed."

She turned to face him, relieved. Her fatigue lightened as she fell into step beside him. "I'm ready for this heat to let up, and we're about to face August," she said as they made their way out onto the hot parking lot.

"I'm with you on that." He gave her a sidelong grin that made her insides flutter.

The short walk to their adjacent vehicles ended too soon. She couldn't even deny to herself the reason she didn't want to part from him. She'd reached a new level of caring, one that bordered on …love. He was attractive, capable and hardworking—all attributes of a worthy life partner. But there was no point in foolish dreaming. He had made it clear he wasn't ready to risk another committed relationship.

Erin stopped at her car as Miles rounded it to his truck. She watched him open the door as she scooted behind her wheel and started the engine. As she backed out of her parking spot, she heard his engine come to life.

Focusing forward, she drove to the exit and glanced back to see his truck begin backing out of its parking spot. She looked both ways and pulled out of the lot into the traffic.

She rolled into the correct lane and picked up speed, glancing in the rearview mirror for sight of Miles. When she didn't see him, she eased off the accelerator to allow him to catch up to her. She'd driven only a hundred yards or so when she glanced in the mirror again and noticed a black car moving up behind her. It had a shiny chrome hood ornament that glinted in the bright sunlight, and it was moving fast.

Alarmed, she glanced in the mirror again, searching for Miles's truck behind it—and not seeing it. And the car was closing the distance between them. Noting on the speedometer that she was already near the speed limit, she pressed the accelerator and surpassed it.

A second later, the car whipped into the next lane and pulled alongside her. Then a bullet slammed through the door window. As glass shattered, another bullet struck. Her head snapped forward onto the steering wheel, and she lost her grip on it.

The world spun as the car swerved, hit the shoulder of the highway and careened alongside it. Then it rolled onto unpaved surface, tipped over and tumbled down the embankment.

~

Miles seethed in frustration. While pulling out of the parking lot, he had heard a sound like knocking or pecking. When the steering wheel jerked to the left, he had pulled to the edge of the road and exited the truck to find both of his rear tires hissing and deflating. It was sabotage.

"Get here as fast as you can," he yelled into the phone at Keaton. "Someone put nail spikes behind my tires. I'm on the side of the road just west of the mall, and Erin's on her way home. I'm sure someone's after her."

"I'm only a mile or so from you, and I'm on my way. Are you off the road enough to leave your truck?"

"Yes. I'll call the police and tell them what's happening. Hurry." His heart was thudding so hard he could scarcely breathe. She had only been gone a minute, but anything could happen in a minute.

He disconnected and made the next call. The police said they would have a car there in less than five minutes.

Miles was angry. But even more, he was scared. For Erin. She was in mortal danger. He knew it in his gut. And he was stranded here—helpless.

He scanned the traffic zooming along the highway, seemingly uncaring that his world was coming apart. Then a thought pierced his brain.

What was it he had heard Erin's dad say during a visit? Suddenly it came to him.

"When you're feeling worried or down—try looking up."

He raised his eyes heavenward. *Please, God. Get me to her in time.*

He paced the road behind his truck and leaped into the car beside Keaton when his colleague rolled to the side of the road. "They're after her," he said loudly as he yanked the door shut and reached for the seat belt. "Those nail spikes make that clear."

He held his breath, scanning the roadside as Keaton drove. It didn't take long to spot her car. It rested at a tilt near the bottom of an embankment, the position telling him it had rolled completely over and come to rest at that angle.

"I'll give the police our location," Keaton said as he braked to a halt above the car.

Miles vaulted to the ground before the car had completely stopped moving. He ran down the embankment, his heart in his throat. When he reached the car door, he wanted to scream in agony, but managed to stifle it. Erin lay slumped beneath the steering wheel, unmoving, her face deathly pale. Blood oozed down her arm.

He jerked the door open and leaned over her, ignoring everything but his need to see her open her eyes, speak to him—be alive.

"Breathe," he ordered in a voice that came out as a whispered squeak.

"Police are coming. I'm calling an ambulance," Keaton said, sliding to a halt behind him.

Miles scanned hurriedly, trying to determine her injuries. Relief threaded through him when he saw that the bullet wound was in her shoulder, not her chest.

"Erin. Can you hear me? Please speak to me." He gently cupped her face in his hands, searching for any sign of life while feeling for a pulse. When he saw her chest move ever so slightly, he inhaled a deep breath of relief. And welcomed the sound of sirens.

"Can you hear me?" he repeated when she didn't respond.

Her eyes fluttered, and then opened partially. "There are two of you," she mumbled.

He searched her face for signs of more injuries—and realized how much she meant to him. Before reason could stop him, he leaned over and kissed her, emotions he couldn't control coursing through him.

The depth of what was happening scared him.

When an ambulance pulled to the side of the highway, he looked back over his shoulder. Two EMTs removed a gurney from the back of the vehicle and began pushing and pulling it down the bumpy embankment.

~

Erin's thoughts were jumbled. Her eyes wouldn't open again.

Her shoulder throbbed with pain.

Miles had come. That meant she was safe.

She sensed EMTs working with her. A blood pressure cuff was wrapped around her uninjured arm.

Had Miles kissed her? It seemed lips had touched hers, breath wafting over her, warm and sweet.

A door slammed closed. Then there was the motion of the ambulance speeding away. Everything faded to darkness.

When she woke, it took several moments for her to orient. She vaguely remembered being prodded and examined. Questioned. Told that her seat belt had prevented further injury.

The curtain around her bed parted, and a face peeked around it at her.

She nearly blubbered at seeing Miles. When he moved through the opening and came to stand at her bedside, a whiff of musky aftershave reached her.

"I called your parents. They're on their way. Are you feeling any better?" A hand moved toward hers, but stopped and pulled back.

"Why is someone still after me?" she asked groggily.

He tugged a chair next to the bed and sank onto it, putting them at eye level. "I'm not sure. Do you feel up to reviewing a bit to see if we can figure that out?"

She started to nod, but stopped at the pain it caused.

He reached over and touched her jaw, traced the hollow under her cheekbone. "Are you sure you're up to it?"

Erin reveled in the sensation of his touch. But then common sense prevailed. She breathed in the antiseptic smell of the room and forced her mind onto the suggested review.

"It all started with that collision with Bike," she said, thinking back. "Well, it didn't actually start until after I found that flash drive."

"And we keep coming back to that," he said, encouraging her to continue.

"I was attacked. And then Bike was killed."

"We think because he lost that flash drive and failed to get it back. He had information about the drug operation on it that he was using in an attempt to blackmail the boss—who we assume is Leland—not realizing the kind of power he was going up against. If our theory is correct, Leland has been after that flash drive to keep anyone from seeing it."

"Which is why someone tried to snatch my purse, thinking the drive was in it. He failed to get it, and was killed," she added quickly, struggling to organize her thoughts.

Miles nodded. "After Dexter Thornton was killed, you were attacked because his killer believed you saw him and could identify him, or that you saw his license plate. I believe that's still the case."

"Before he could get rid of me, Leland was named as the boss and arrested, but now he's out on bail and can't be found," she continued, her eyes only partially open. "He must have hired a killer to take out Bike and Dexter. Whoever he hired could be hiding him. So we're no closer to answers than we were," she concluded, disappointed at another merry-go-round of fact chasing. She forced her eyes fully open.

Miles shrugged. "That's how we eventually figure out cases, going over and over what we know and hitting on a missed detail that leads to an answer. We just have to keep doing it until that happens."

The door eased open, and Erin's parents stepped inside, their faces reflecting worry. Everett led Verna to the bedside, and Erin reached over to clasp her mother's outstretched hand. "I'm okay, Mom, Dad. I'll be out of here in no time."

Verna leaned over and hugged her gently. "You follow doctor's orders and leave only when you're told you can."

Everett glanced over at Miles. "Doctors make terrible patients, I've heard." He took his turn hugging Erin. "Listen to your mom. She's right."

Miles shook hands with the man. "I'm glad you're here. You need some privacy with your daughter, and I need to go to the third floor and visit with a teen drug user who overdosed. My partner called as I was on my way here and suggested I see the guy after visiting with Erin."

Erin frowned. "The drugs are still flowing then?"

He scowled. "Apparently Bike's list didn't cover all the vendors involved. There must be more—and they're foolhardy enough to keep pushing the stuff."

"Greed will make people take foolish chances."

He nodded and left.

Chapter 16

Miles deliberated as he walked to the elevator, stepped inside it and rode to the third floor. He was worried about Erin, how to keep her safe. And how to deal with his feelings for her. He couldn't attach the word love to them. It was too dangerous. Keeping his personal and professional lives separate had reached a blurry line.

After Shelly's death he had thought he would remain single the rest of his life. He had even reached the point of— maybe not enjoyment—but satisfaction with the freedom that came with that. All thoughts of having a wife and family had been pushed from his mind.

Until he met Erin.

Since then, his life had spiraled out of control.

Memories of Shelly never went away. But with the passing of time the blinding pain had gradually dulled. He had learned to concentrate on the pleasant memories rather than the grief. Knowing that she was in heaven gave him comfort.

The whoosh of the elevator door opening brought him back to the task at hand.

When he entered the hospital room of Lance Dansby, the teen suffering from an overdose, he saw a couple who had to be his parents seated near the bed. The man stood and directed a suspicious look at Miles. "Who are you?"

"I'm Agent Miles Jarrett, DEA." He showed the man his badge. "May I assume you two are this young man's parents?"

The man nodded, visibly unhappy at the intrusion into their private family time.

"I need to ask your son some questions."

The woman moved to her husband's side. "This has gotten too big for us, Bill. Let the man talk to Lance. Those drug suppliers have to be stopped."

Miles was afraid the boy would just find another source, if he survived and was addicted. But he wasn't about to voice such a thought.

When the man reluctantly accompanied his wife back to their seats, Miles stepped over next to the bed. The young man was pale. An oxygen mask covered his face, monitors above the bed beeped.

"Lance, I need you to tell me who sold you the drugs."

Dark eyes peered at him from above the mask. "I'm not telling you, or any cop, anything."

"That's not smart, Lance. Those drugs are destroying your life and grieving your parents. Helping me could help you."

The boy's eyes darted to the parents. But he didn't speak.

"I'm sure they love you and don't want you to come to a bad end. Please think of them."

The boy remained silent for so long that Miles had nearly given up hope when he finally spoke. "I don't know names. You just say the right words and are told where to go in the parking lot. It's not always the same one."

That jived with what they already knew, but it didn't provide any new leads. "Is there anything else, anything at all that you can give me?"

The young man glanced at his parents again, questioning. When his mother nodded, he looked back at Miles. "I don't know if it means anything, but one time I saw a sticky note on a woman dealer's table that said Trouble Hot Line, and it had a phone number on it."

Hope sparked, even though it was a long shot. "Can you remember the number?"

The boy closed his eyes, squeezing them in thought. Then they popped open again. "All I remember is that the last four digits were almost all the same number. I remember there were three numbers alike and one different, but I don't remember if there were more twos than threes or more threes than twos."

Miles whipped out a notepad and jotted down the combinations. "Do you remember the area code and prefix?"

Lance told him, and Miles added it to his notes.

"That's all I know," the young man said, closing his eyes.

Miles thanked him, nodded at the older couple and left the room. After he exited the hospital, he drove directly to his apartment and contacted Julian.

"I'll work with different combinations and get back to you as soon as possible," Julian promised after being given the numbers to work with in a trace.

As soon as he disconnected, Miles scrounged in the refrigerator for something to stop the growling in his stomach. He ended up making an omelet and some strong coffee.

When he had finished eating and was clearing up the kitchen, Julian called back. "I found a number that fits, but you're not going to like where that phone is located," he warned when Miles answered.

"Spit it out."

"It's a land line in Senator Fielder's office."

"Okay, thanks. I'll be doing some research of my own now."

As he disconnected, Miles reached over and booted his laptop. Could the note with that number have been dropped by someone totally unrelated to the drugs? The senator and his campaigners had been in the mall. Questions and possibilities hammered at him.

After devoting the rest of the evening to locating and reading everything he could find about Fielder, Miles had found a lot of information—and none of it negative.

The senator seemed to have connections to a lot of worthy causes and community events. He served on the board of a rehab facility and belonged to a number of political organizations. His reputation was top notch. Did he have a staffer who was involved in the drug business?

Finally, exhausted and at a dead end, Miles called it a night, showered and went to bed.

The next morning, he went to the hospital first thing, anxious to check on Erin. When he opened the door to her room, he stood staring at her still form in the bed, sleeping. There was strength behind her beauty. She was tough. He knew that. But right now there was nothing tough about her. She was vulnerable, and that very vulnerability drew him to her. A pang of tenderness nearly overwhelmed him.

As he advanced into the room, she stirred, and then opened her eyes. She smiled. "Have you come to spring me from this place?"

"No one's springing you until a doctor releases you."

Erin sat up in the bed, her arm held in place by a sling. "Mom called Lydia last night and told her to cancel my appointments for today, but I plan to be out of here this afternoon and back in the office tomorrow morning."

He dropped onto a chair. "Has a doctor agreed?"

She nodded. "I talked to him earlier this morning."

"He wasn't happy about it, but gave in under pressure, huh?"

She shrugged. "Something like that. My parents are going to pick me up after lunch."

A pang of disappointment struck him. He would have liked that privilege. But this might be a better answer. "Are they taking you home with them?"

Her look turned a tad sheepish. "Yes, that was what got the doctor to agree. He also understands about my patients."

"Good." He breathed easier. "I'll come get you tomorrow morning and bring you to work. You don't need to be driving with that arm injury."

She winced, her free hand rubbing along the sling. "I also don't have a car. Have you found out who shot me?" she asked before he could comment on the car.

He leaned forward in the chair. "Unfortunately, we haven't. Whoever it was, he left no clues other than the bullet removed from your shoulder. But I did find out something interesting from that teenager I went to see when I left you last night."

"You mean the one who overdosed?"

He nodded and explained about the phone number.

"Wow," she said when he finished. "The congressman is back and forth between the capital and his home all the time, so he's not in that office a lot. It's a big building, so anyone could be set up in there and him not know about it."

"I'm leaning toward a campaign worker, someone involved in the community and political scene—and more."

"Like a hit man," she added somberly.

His phone interrupted their speculations. It was the police detective. "Jarrett."

He listened to what the investigator had to tell him. Then he smiled. "That's good to hear. Thanks for letting me know."

When he disconnected, he looked at Erin again. "That was the local detective. He said they've arrested the teens accessing pictures from the cameras in the dressing rooms and bathrooms. Under questioning, it was also determined that two of them by the names of Jack and Dooley are the ones who hurt Freddy. He thought they were his friends."

Erin perked up a bit. "Did they claim to be making porn films on their own, or admit that they're working for someone?"

"You ask a lot of questions for someone in a hospital bed."

She managed a semblance of a smile. "My brain isn't in a sling."

He chuckled. "One of them admitted that they're working for Leland Zink."

"So he's a multi-entrepreneur."

"And his whereabouts are unknown." Miles stood, dropped a kiss on her forehead and left.

~

"You're scaring years off my life," Ginger said as she dropped onto the sofa next to Erin.

"I'm sorry about that." Erin gave her head a rueful shake. "I assure you I'd prefer that not be the case."

Ginger eyed Erin in medical scrutiny. "First, you bring me a security guard for treatment of injuries. Then you start having scary incidents happen to you. And now you end up in the hospital from a shooting. What's going on? And why did I have to hear about it from someone else?"

Ginger had driven down here to Ozark from work after someone told her about a news report. Erin felt guilty at not having contacted her personally.

"I didn't want to scare years off your life," she said, giving her friend an apologetic wince.

Ginger made a nod of understanding. "I guess I get it. You didn't feel good, and you didn't want me to worry. Are you ready to tell me the whole story now?"

Erin nodded, needing a sympathetic ear.

Verna entered the room, two cold sodas in her hands. Dad followed right behind her with two glasses filled with ice cubes. "Do you girls need liquid sustenance?" she asked.

When both indicated they did, the couple set the drinks and glasses on the coffee table. "Now we'll go sit on the back porch while you visit," Mom announced with a smile.

"We're so glad you came by, Ginger. Hopefully you can talk some sense into Erin," Dad said. "Convince her to stay with us until this—whatever it is—is over."

With that, they headed to the porch.

"He's right," Ginger said, pouring soda into the glasses. "Now give me a full explanation of what's been happening to you—and why."

Erin sipped from her soda, replaced the glass and leaned back against the sofa. She adjusted the sling and arm to a more comfortable position. "Okay."

And she did. Over the next several minutes, she went over the events of the past three weeks, beginning with the collision in the parking lot and ending with the shooting that had landed her in the hospital.

When she finished, Ginger sat staring at her. "Wow," she said at last. "You landed in a real mess, didn't you? Tell me more about Miles," she continued without waiting for a response. "He's more than just a friend to you, isn't he?"

Erin wanted to deny it, but couldn't. "Circumstances have caused us to spend a lot of time together. And I admit I like him."

Ginger nodded. "I see. And would I be correct in thinking there's more to his presence in the mall than just being a security guard?"

"He's a DEA agent, and he's been working undercover to stop the drug operation at the flea market."

"Your story makes more sense now. You said the market owner is one of the two men who have disappeared. Are they suspected of running the drug operation?"

"I'm not sure about Mark Hammond. He seems to be more of an enforcer. I think Leland is the one the police believe is behind it all."

Ginger tapped a finger gently on her lips, frowning. "What's Leland's last name?"

"Zink."

Her eyes widened. "I know him. We grew up in the same neighborhood."

Surprised, Erin replaced the glass she had picked up, intending to take a drink. "Do you think he's the type of guy who would sell drugs, not caring who they hurt? Not that I know what *type* would do such a thing," she added, feeling guilty for putting the question that way.

Ginger shrugged. "He was kind of rowdy, but it was just small scrapes that landed him in trouble from time to time."

Ginger stared across the room, as if not seeing anything, but deep in contemplation. Then she continued, speaking slowly. "There was that summer when he was about fourteen or fifteen. He spent two or three weeks with a relative, and they got into some trouble I think was big."

"What kind of trouble?"

"That's what I'm trying to remember." Her brows furrowed in concentration. "I think there was a wreck. Yes, that's it." She snapped her fingers. "He and a cousin were riding a motorcycle and hit a car. The driver was thrown from his car and died from his injuries. Leland was secretive when he returned home and was asked about it. I never saw any news stories about it."

Now Erin frowned. "Do you think there was a cover-up?"

"Maybe. I don't know. The only time I ever heard anyone ask Leland about it, he just said he wasn't supposed to talk about it."

"So something could have been swept under the rug. Do you recall the cousin's name?"

Ginger went into thoughtful mode again. "Leland used to brag about having some relatives who were so rich that they could do whatever they wanted. He joked about his mom's cousins who were once removed, or something like that. Anyhow, he mentioned this one cousin, second or third I think, who was the same age as Leland, and how much fun they had when they were able to spend time together. It seems like he said they lived in Springfield at the time."

Intrigued, Erin leaned forward. "What was that cousin's name?"

Ginger thought for several moments, and then a hand went over her mouth, her pupils dilated above it. "Ray," she said faintly. "Ray Fielder."

Erin's thoughts went into a tailspin. Then she began to verbalize them. "Leland owns the flea market, and vendors who have been arrested say they work for him. After he was arrested and made bail, a phone number was traced to a phone in the building where Ray has his campaign headquarters. Leland must have an office there. He doesn't have one at the mall."

As questions flooded her brain, little warning bells clanged. Did Leland still spend time with his rich cousin? Could he ask favors of him when he needed help? A place to hide? Did the senator know his cousin could be running a drug business in the mall and have an office in his office building?

"It sounds like your brain is functioning," Ginger said, picking up her soda. After sipping from it while getting no response, she backed away from the subject, and they spent a few more minutes visiting. But the earlier conversation about Leland returned to Erin's mind as soon as Ginger was gone. She had to tell Miles about it. But she hesitated, something else nagging at the back of her mind.

As her parents returned to the room, the photos on that flash drive came to mind. She couldn't shake the feeling that she needed to look at them again, study them in more detail. If Bike had been trying to blackmail Leland with the files and photos on it, there had to be more meaning hidden behind them.

She eased up off the sofa, being careful of her arm.

"Are you going to bed so early?" her dad asked, concern in his voice.

Erin shook her head. "No, I'm going to read for a while, see if I can relax." Well, it *was* reading, even if it wasn't the relaxing kind.

Once in the room her parents still kept as it had been when Erin lived there permanently, she booted her laptop and opened the flash drive.

She looked at that list again, but could detect no further clues in it. So she turned her attention to the photos, studying them one by one. After staring at them so long her vision blurred, she leaned back in the chair and closed her eyes. The pictures were just random shots of scenery, buildings and objects.

As she remained still and quiet, visual images began to flow through her mind, depicting each step of her involvement in this mess. When her mental film reel reached the point of her purse snatcher's murder, she recalled seeing the killer at his car, his face and hair obscured, his eyes shaded. And a shudder ran through her.

Suddenly she went rigid as her thoughts veered from the killer thinking she had seen enough of his body to recognize him, to the theory that he was afraid she had seen his license plate and could identify his car. She bolted upright in the chair and leaned forward to study the pictures some more. There were several shots of vehicles among them. And scanning through them revealed that the license plates were visible in every one of them.

Was that what the photographs were about? Did they in some way suggest the identity of persons involved in the drug dealing? Was Bike letting Leland know that he knew who they were, and that he would give the information to the police if his blackmail demand was not met?

Now she grabbed her phone to call Miles.

Chapter 17

Miles was pleased when he checked his phone ID and saw that it was Erin calling. When she explained what she had noted on the flash drive, his hopes sparked. He grabbed a pen and notepad and jotted down the numbers as she quoted them. "I'll run those plates and get right back to you."

As soon as they disconnected, he began. And when he had the results listed, he couldn't call Erin back. He had to talk to her face to face. He pocketed the paper with the list of plate numbers and their owners and headed out the door.

When he knocked at the door of her parents' house, her dad opened it. Alarm flashed across his face when he recognized Miles. "Is something wrong?"

"No, I just returned so soon because I have some information I want to show Erin. Has she already gone to bed?"

Everett stepped back, opening the door wider. "I don't think so, but she's in her room. Come on in, and I'll call her." The man seemed genuinely pleased to see him. And that genuinely pleased Miles. Which it shouldn't.

"Erin," the man called at the hallway. "There's someone here to see you."

Moments later, Erin entered the room, her expression a mixture of pleasure and alarm. "What did you find?"

Miles took the list from his pocket and handed it to her. "I wanted to see your face when you read this." A quick glance around the room told him that her dad had left them alone.

She read intently. When she looked up, she blew out a whoosh of breath. "It's proof. Those cars belong to the four vendors already identified, plus the one who sells cleaning supplies."

He nodded. "When I leave here, I'll contact Keaton and make plans to arrest that guy in the morning. Do you still have your computer booted?"

She nodded. "What do you have in mind?"

"On the drive down here, I was thinking that maybe we ought to study those pictures together. After the way you picked up on the significance of those plates, maybe there's something else we've missed."

She stared at him for a moment, and then her mouth spread into a wide grin. "Let's do it."

She beckoned for him to follow her. "This was my room growing up," she said once inside the room that doubled as a bedroom and an office. Neatly organized, it was done in restful colors of cream and pastel blue. A desk and chair occupied a corner section of the room, a laptop open on the desk.

"I'll get another chair." She motioned for him to take the one at the desk.

Miles sat and stared at the screen where she had left the file open. He was looking close, studying one picture after another when she returned, set a kitchen chair next to him and sank onto it. The pleasant floral scent he associated with her wafted to him.

Forcing himself to concentrate, he peered at the picture of a dark SUV. The license plate was visible but blurry. He pointed at it. "Is that one of the plates you were able to read?"

She shook her head. "No, it was too blurry."

He tried again to read it. "Julian might be able to enhance the picture and make out the numbers." He pulled out his phone and called the tech expert.

"Send me the picture, and I'll give it a try," Julian said after hearing what Miles needed. "I'm not at work so don't have access to the file, but my equipment here at home is good. I'll call you right back if I have any luck."

Miles disconnected and sent the photo. Then he faced Erin. "Now we wait."

"Would you like some coffee or a cold drink?"

"No, but thanks for the offer." He looked at the screen again and focused on the entire image he had just sent to Julian. "Look at this." He pointed at the number on the front of the stately house behind that SUV. "Can you make out that address number?"

Erin peered at it, squinting. "That's a one at the end of the digits. And the third one looks like it could be a two. The second looks like a zero. But I can't tell if the first one is an eight or a three. Or it might be a five."

Miles grinned, picking up the pen that lay on her desk. He jotted the various combinations onto the list from his pocket. Then he began searching for matches. The first name he found was unfamiliar, but he made a note of it. Then he tried another combination. And another. Then he whistled and leaned back.

Erin's expression lit with anticipation.

"That house may be the senator's."

As he spoke, his phone rang. It was Julian. "Yeah."

"Do you want the enhanced picture, or should I just give you the number I got?"

"Give me the number. Then send the enhancement to me."

Miles wrote it down as Julian cited it, thanked him and disconnected. Then he immediately ran the plate.

"Bingo," he said when he got a name. "That SUV belongs to Leland Zink. And it's parked in front of the senator's house. I have to find the man—and the sooner the better."

Erin frowned. "What are you thinking?"

He drew a deep breath. "My thinking isn't real clear, but there's a very bad feeling growing in my gut."

~

Erin thought she understood. "Leland and Mark both need to be found. Do you think they'll hurt the senator, or are they just asking for help from Leland's rich relative?"

"I'm not sure."

Another thing troubled her. "How do you think they always know where to find me?"

He frowned. "They're getting tips from someone. I wish I knew who."

She did, too.

When Miles moved to leave, she accompanied him out onto the front porch. Late summer smells mingled with ones that drifted from the house.

"We make a good team," he said, facing her. "I know you plan to go back to work in the morning. I won't argue about that, but I don't think you should drive. I'll come get you and bring you back. You still need protection," he added.

She shrugged, too uncertain to protest.

Reaching out, he gently cupped her cheek. "Does that mean you agree?"

She nodded—and didn't offer a word of protest when he bent his head and brushed her lips with his in a sweet, gentle kiss. It was so right that she didn't want it to end.

After a long, wonderful moment, he pulled away, though. And stood gazing at her in the glow of the porch light. "I never thought I'd feel this way again. I wish I didn't have to leave. But it's late."

Erin smiled. "I'll be waiting for you in the morning."

He grinned and headed down the steps.

She watched him climb into his truck and drive away, her heart still beating a little too fast. Love had come to her unexpectedly. She didn't know how she was going to survive when Miles left.

~

The next morning, Miles drove to Ozark after Erin and delivered her to work, not bothering to question her decision to ditch her sling. He understood her need for freedom of movement to do her work. She would deal with the pain.

He tried to ignore the way having her near him set his heart racing. He had crossed a line last night. And he didn't know what to do about it.

The woman was giving him heart trouble. Those attacks on her were causing near heart attacks. And being with her— kissing her—was nearly as scary.

As he turned into the mall parking lot, he shoved a mental barrier in place and locked the thoughts behind it. After escorting Erin to her office, he entered the mall and took a stroll around the flea market. No longer in uniform, no one paid him any attention.

He stared at the still closed mobile phone booth, the table now empty. He looked up the regular security guard and asked him about it.

Charlie peered over at the spot. "It was empty when I came on duty this morning. Last night's guard said somebody came in last night, boxed up everything and hauled it out."

Miles thanked him and returned to his truck for privacy. He called Julian. "Can you pull up those prints I took from the mobile phone booth and run them against criminal databases? See if either of them gets a match."

"I'll see what I can do," the technician promised. "Should I be looking for anything in particular?"

"I need to find Mark Hammond. He's out of business here at the mall, but he's on the loose and dangerous. I think he's our killer, and he needs to be stopped before there are more hits."

"I'm on it."

Debating what to do next, Miles contacted Keaton. "Where are you?"

"I'm having brunch and coffee," his partner answered, naming the restaurant. "Why don't you join me? We can rehash things and compare notes, decide how to wrap up this case."

"I'll be there in five to ten minutes."

A half hour later, while Miles was eating an omelet, Miles's phone rang. It was Julian. "Jarrett."

"Got a hit," he announced. "The guy uses several aliases. One of them is Ron Kinzer."

Miles grinned across the table at Keaton, who had set his coffee mug down to listen. He spoke quietly, not wanting his voice to carry in the restaurant. "That's the name he used to text orders for Bike to get *it* back. He must have a second phone in that name."

"Here's the kicker, though," Julian continued. "That print also matches to a Mark Halloran. I think Mark Hammond is just his most recent alias. Mark Halloran is the real deal. He has a violent history with an ex-wife, and other criminal charges. He served time on the ex-wife charge, and she went into hiding when he was released. That's all I have for now."

"Can you trace his cell phone and see if you can get a location?"

"I'll see what I can do."

Miles disconnected and made eye contact with Keaton. "Did you follow that?"

Keaton nodded. "Enough to know that Hammond is Leland's hired killer."

"I think I need to go back to the mall and keep an eye on Erin's office," Miles decided aloud. "He's after her, and she can't stay inside that office indefinitely."

Keaton grinned, but he nodded agreement.

They finished eating, paid their bills and headed out of the building. Both their phones pinged as they stepped out onto the parking lot.

Simultaneously, they reached for them. Read the text. And their gazes met. "We're too late," Keaton said in a half moan.

"And wrong about who's the boss."

The message was a group text from the police detective notifying them that he was headed to the site where a body had been found—and tentatively identified as Leland Zink.

"Leland may have been the boss of the mall operation," Keaton said grimly, "but he's not the TOP boss."

Miles nodded. "Whoever that is, he's more powerful and deadly, and anyone who crosses him, or messes up, is killed."

"And Hammond—I mean Halloran—is working for him, not Leland as we had thought," Keaton concluded.

They headed to their vehicles.

~

Erin stared in horror at the text from Miles.

We're at a site where Leland Zink's body was found. DO NOT leave your office. I'll be there soon as I can.

The nightmare had worsened rather than getting better. Her mind whirling at warp speed, she collapsed onto the chair behind her desk, thankful she had been here in her private office when her phone pinged.

Why did these things keep happening?

Who was behind them?

How did someone always know how to find anyone they wanted dead? How?

Information was being provided by someone with access to it. Some of it was from outside sources—maybe even from someone in the police department. But most of it seemed to have come from inside the mall.

Erin searched her memory, frantic for answers. Leaning forward on her elbows, her hands went over her face. In the darkness behind her eyelids, she prayed. *Help me, Lord. Please.*

A measure of calm settled over her, giving her more clarity of thought. She recalled the morning of the failed DEA raid. Could that have been her fault? She had known about the plan to conduct it. So far as she knew, no one else had. Suddenly it occurred to her that one other person *had* known about her cancelled appointments and whereabouts that morning. Her assistant.

Could Lydia have sensed something and leaked that information? Would she? If so, how would she have known about the raid? As the questions hammered at her brain, Erin recalled speaking to Miles on the phone about it.

She pushed to her feet, an idea forming. In growing horror, her gaze visually inspected the entire office. Nothing was new, and she didn't note anything out of place.

She began to walk slowly around the room, studying the shelves, light fixtures and furnishings. Then she returned to her desk and checked underneath it. Nothing.

But as she came upright from her stooped position, her gaze swept over the electrical outlet about eighteen inches above the floor behind the desk. She squatted and studied it more closely. It looked okay, but something seemed off. What looked like a dab of powdered sugar lay on the floor beneath it. And the color of the plate was the tiniest bit darker than the others in the room.

Leaning closer, she detected what she thought looked like a transmitter. Horror grew at the realization that her office had been bugged. And only one person could have done it.

Stunned, she stood and plopped back onto her desk chair.

Why? What was Lydia's motive, her connection to all this?

Sick at heart, and screaming inside with anger, Erin tried to think.

I need more help, Lord. Please guide me to the answer.

Ever so slowly she regained another semblance of calm. And her mind focused on Lydia. Her work performance. Her personal habits. Anything she could recall about her assistant.

Lydia was organized. Efficient. A bit quirky at times. The only thing Erin could recall seeing the least bit messy was her desk calendar with doodles all over it. She pictured it as it had been the evening she had returned to the mall with Miles after finding Archie in his truck and being directed to that hideout. That evening was when she had called Miles and spoken to him about the planned raid. Then she had gone to Lydia's desk and called to have her cancel the next morning's appointments.

As the scene replayed in her mind, she again recalled the cartoonish doodles on that desk pad. The largest one had been of a heart drawn near the top right corner of it. There had been initials inside it, drawn in beautiful calligraphy. She paused. What had those initials been?

Erin didn't know much about Lydia's personal life. She lived in an apartment only a couple of miles away and had a cat she called Muffy. Her family lived in a suburb a few miles east of Springfield, and she visited them occasionally. But she never spoke of a special man in her life.

Erin assumed she dated. The initials in that heart seemed to indicate she did.

Concentrating fiercely, Erin tried to visualize that heart in her mind's eye. It was blurry, but when she pictured the flourishes and how they looked, she thought she had it. "R. F.," she murmured to herself as the vision became clearer. "R. F."

She went rigid as a name came to her. That couldn't possibly mean Ray Fielder, could it? The senator? No way.

But then she recalled something else. The senator had made an appearance at the mall the morning after those arrests. Then Lydia had suddenly needed to leave work early that day. If there was a connection, could there have been a rendezvous?

Erin enumerated rapidly. The bug in her office. The raid. The insignificant early departure from the office that day.

She wasn't sure why, or what else might be involved, but Lydia had to be the leak.

Lydia would be leaving the office within the next five or ten minutes. She couldn't be allowed to go. She might figure out she was caught and take off. But how could she be kept here? Erin had to find out for sure about her assistant's involvement.

And she had to let Miles know what she knew. She grabbed her phone and sent him a text.

Chapter 18

Miles fought panic when he read Erin's text. He stepped over next to Keaton and showed it to him.

My assistant is the leak. Office bugged. Can't let her leave.

"You have to go," Keaton declared. "Don't worry about this. I'll take care of it."

Miles scanned the crime scene. They were inside a house outside the city limits of Springfield, and the forensics team was still collecting evidence. Leland Zink's body lay beneath a black cover. He had been shot, presumably here in the living room. The stench of blood permeated the air. Outside, yellow tape surrounded the perimeter of the house.

"Thanks." He headed to his truck at a run.

He made it halfway to the mall in good time, but groaned in frustration when traffic ground to a halt because of an accident up ahead.

He looked around, searching for a way to get moving. Seeing none, he backed up a few inches and shifted the angle of his truck. When the driver of another vehicle glared at him, he flashed his badge in the window. The driver nodded understanding and eased over to create a little more space so

Miles could maneuver onto the shoulder of the highway. He waved a thank-you, made a U-turn and rolled away.

He made it to a spot where he could get back onto the highway and sped onto a side road parallel to the highway.

Then he rammed the accelerator to the floorboard.

~

Erin cradled her arm to ease the pressure on her sore shoulder, speed debating how to make sure Lydia didn't leave the office. She headed for the little kitchen, thinking as she went. She opened the refrigerator and grabbed the pitcher of tea left over from her lunch. Then she hastily dumped ice cubes in two glasses and poured tea over them.

Carrying the glasses, she went to the doorway of Lydia's office and raised them in front of her. "I need you to come to my office to discuss a couple of things before you leave." She struggled for normalcy in her voice.

Lydia looked up from tidying her desk, her eyewear for the day consisting of thin, lightweight, round metal frames. She eyed the tea thirstily. "I'll be right there."

Erin proceeded to her desk and set one of the glasses on it, the other on the little table near a chair next to the door.

When Lydia arrived, she plunked down in the chair by the little table, which put her facing Erin at an angle, her whitish blond hair hanging loosely around her neck. She took a quick sip of tea and placed the glass back on the table. "Ah, that was good. How's your shoulder?"

Erin shrugged, resisting the urge to rub it. "It's sore, but doing fine. I appreciate you taking care of things yesterday." She nearly choked on the words, thinking why she hadn't been there. Now she went for the jugular. "When did you plant that bug in here?" She pointed at the plate on the wall.

Taken totally off guard, Lydia's jaw dropped, a brief flicker of panic in her eyes. For a moment she sat frozen in place. Then those blue eyes narrowed into an ominous glare, her carefully made up face twisting into a knot of fury.

She came off the chair and advanced toward the desk. "You find something in your office, and you automatically blame me because I'm convenient, is that it?"

"I believe you did it some time ago and have been spying on me, and then passing along information." Erin stood, meaning to hold her ground.

Suddenly Lydia lunged forward and grabbed the letter opener from the desktop. She raised it in the air. As it plunged downward, Erin shoved the desk forward as hard as she could, the force tipping her body backward.

As Lydia crashed into it and tumbled backward, Erin searched frantically for something to use for self-defense. The first thing that hit her vision was the shelf of medicines above where Lydia had fallen. She snatched two plastic bottles from it and threw them at Lydia, who was scrambling to her feet. One hit her in the neck, causing her to lose her balance and stumble backward. But she quickly regained her equilibrium and launched forward in a flying tackle that caught Erin in the midriff. They landed in a tangle of arms and legs, rolling across the carpet until they hit the edge of the desk with a thud.

Arms flailing, Lydia caught Erin in the cheek with an elbow, making her see stars. As her hand went reflexively to her face, Lydia scrambled to her knees. Then she lunged to one side and raked a hand over the carpet. She came up with the letter opener she had dropped—and once again raised it.

~

As he raced inside the front office of Erin's vision center, Miles heard sounds of a disturbance coming from the back. He ran across the room, into the hallway and toward Erin's private office—and the sounds. When he shoved the door open, his heart nearly stopped beating at the sight of Lydia, kneeling above Erin, a pointed weapon raised to stab her.

As Lydia's arm began its plunge, he propelled his body forward in a flying leap, his arm swinging at hers. The weapon went flying, and Lydia toppled onto her side. Erin began scooting backward like a crab, away from her.

Miles grabbed Lydia's wrist and hauled her to her feet. "You have the right to remain silent," he quoted. "Anything you say may be held against you. You have the right to an attorney. If you …"

"Shut up!" Lydia screamed, jerking wildly in an effort to escape his grip. "Just shut up. You have no reason to arrest me."

"I just walked in on you attempting to kill your employer. And you're feeding illegally obtained information to people trying to kill her."

Icy coldness settled in his veins at the thought of what it would have done to him if they had succeeded.

He steered the assistant backward and down onto the chair near the wall, checking peripherally to see that Erin had made it to her feet. She stood next to her desk, a dazed look on her face. He motioned for her to sit.

When Erin had dropped onto her desk chair, he perched on the edge of the desk and faced Lydia again. "Now let's talk. Who are you feeding information to?"

Lydia's smirk made him sick to his stomach. Her gaze darted around the room, seeking a way to escape. "You have no right to question me."

"Yes, I do. I'm Agent Miles Jarrett, DEA. And you're about to take the fall for your boss—or bosses."

She crossed her arms and glared at him in defiance. "You don't have anything on me."

"Oh, but we do. For starters, I just witnessed you attempting to kill your boss. And when we finish our investigation, you'll be doing time for the murders of Harley Davis, Dexter Thornton and Leland Zink."

Her head jerked upward. "I didn't kill those guys."

"But you know who did, and your involvement will land you in prison. Once the whole drug operation is shut down, you'll be on your own. Your comrades will turn on you."

When the bravado began to visibly leak out of her, he forged ahead. "Admit you bugged your boss's office. I'm sure your prints will be found inside that transmitter plate." He indicated it with a head motion.

"Okay, I admit it," she yelped angrily.

"And you told the hit man how to find Erin."

"Yes."

"And you tipped them off about the raid we planned."

She only nodded, her expression one of hatred.

He kept pushing, afraid she was about to shut down. "The only thing that might help you is if you tell us what you know. Why were Davis and Thornton killed?"

She considered for a few moments, wavering, before sneering and speaking in a sour tone. "Bike was blackmailing Leland. He thought he was the boss. He messed up when he lost that copy of his blackmail information and then failed to get it back. So he was taken out and Dexter was sent to get it. He messed up, too."

"What about Leland Zink? How did he mess up?"

"He was in charge of the drug operation, but he started doing the porn on his own, without permission. He acted stupid and jeopardized everything."

"So anyone who crosses the boss dies. Is that right?"

She shrugged, glowering.

"Who's the boss?"

She went still. Then a calculating look came over her face. "Mark Hammond."

"Who's his hit man?"

"He does his own hitting."

"Who do the initials R. F. represent?" Erin spoke up so suddenly they both looked back at her in surprise.

Lydia started to rise, but Miles noticed and stepped in front of her before she could make a break for the door. "Answer the question."

She eased back onto the chair. "It's a dumb question. I don't know."

Miles glanced at Erin for follow-up.

She looked Lydia directly in the eye. "Then why are those initials doodled inside a heart drawn on your desk calendar, the way a girl does when she has a crush on someone? Is there any chance those initials stand for Ray Fielder? Are you the married senator's side dish?"

"No!" Lydia shot to her feet, but sank back down when Miles stepped toward her, gave her a stern look and pointed at the chair. "I'm not a side dish. I'm his main dish. He loves me. His wife's a bimbo. He's going to divorce her and marry me."

"Do you think having a high profile lover will keep you out of jail?" Erin shot back at her. "If so, think again. He'll drop you like a hot rock as soon as he hears you've been arrested."

Lydia's mouth twisted. "You have no proof. And I'll just deny everything in court."

Miles smiled. "That's okay. We have all this on tape—thanks to you."

Her eyes rounded in shock as she comprehended that he referred to the bug she had put in this office.

She went pale.

Miles gripped her arm. "Let's go."

As he spoke, a phone rang. He looked over at Erin as she pulled hers from her pocket and answered it. He stayed rooted in place when he saw a horrified expression come over her face.

Chapter 19

Erin's hand trembled so much she could hardly hold the phone. All the voice had said was, "I have your mom," but the menacing words had struck terror in her heart.

"Who are you?" she managed to say past her fear constricted throat.

"That doesn't matter. If you want her to stay alive, you'll come where I tell you and take her place, an even exchange."

"Where?"

"There's another cabin in Rockaway Beach, about a half mile past where that one exploded. Be here in an hour. And come alone. Or she dies." The line went dead.

"What is it?" Miles asked, while dividing his attention between her and Lydia.

"Someone has my mother. He wants me in exchange for her." As she spoke, a smirk appeared at the corners of Lydia's mouth.

Miles must have seen it as well, because he hauled her to her feet. "Let's go."

Erin grabbed her purse and followed him out of the office, keeping silent as he practically dragged Lydia out into the hall. Erin hurriedly locked the office door, and then Miles tossed her his phone. "Call Charlie and ask where he is. I'll have him guard our prisoner until the police can come get her."

Realizing he didn't want to risk losing his grip on Lydia, Erin found Charlie in his listings and dialed. "Where can we find you?" she asked when he answered.

"I'm in the east hallway," he responded. "Where are you? I'll meet you." Apparently sensing the urgency in her voice, and recognizing that the phone belonged to Miles, he was reacting in cop mode.

"We're just leaving the vision center." Her breath had turned shallow.

Within moments, the security guard came running around the corner at the end of the hallway. As they met, Erin's phone rang. It was her dad. She swallowed the terror choking her and answered. "Hi, Dad."

"I can't find your mother," he shouted, more frantic than she had ever heard him. Then he spoke a bit quieter. "She went out in the yard, like she does when it's pretty outside. When she stayed longer than usual, I got worried and went out to check on her. She's gone!"

"Dad," she said as calmly as she could, her voice strained, "I need you to be calm and pray. I'm on my way to get her."

There was a moment of silence. "Are you saying something has happened to her?"

Erin drew to a halt as Miles spoke to the guard and turned Lydia over to him. When he beckoned, Erin followed him. "I don't have time to explain right now, Dad, but I'll get back to you as soon as I can. Please pray, like you always taught others to do."

She disconnected and picked up the pace, her pulse pounding as she raced with Miles to the parking lot. When he started toward his truck, she grabbed his arm. "I should drive my car. He told me to come alone."

It was easy to see he didn't like the idea, but accepted her point. "Tell me exactly what the caller said," he instructed as they hurried to her car.

"A man said he has my mother, and he wants me in exchange for her. He's at a cabin in Rockaway Beach, about a half mile past the one that blew up, and he said be there in an hour."

Miles pulled out his phone. "I told Charlie to have the police come for Lydia, but I need to request backup from the police down at Rockaway." He dialed as they climbed into her car, and then explained the situation and location to someone, emphasizing the time squeeze. He disconnected and reached for his seat belt as she started the engine and zipped out of her parking spot.

"They said they'll have a car meet us at the city limits and follow us to the cabin," he said as she steered into highway traffic.

During the drive, they debated how to approach the situation. "I don't like the idea of you meeting him alone," Miles finally said with reluctance, "but I'm afraid he'll hurt your mother if he sees me. So here's what I want you to do. As soon as we get close to that cabin, slow down enough for me to jump out of the car. Then stall for time as much as you can to give me time to get there and circle around to the back door. There has to be one."

Erin nodded, watching the road as they passed Branson and then approached Rockaway Beach. When they spotted the police car waiting beside the road for them, Miles lowered the passenger window and leaned out to wave his badge at the two officers. The one in the passenger seat waved recognition, and the one behind the wheel steered onto the highway behind them. The car stayed close as Erin followed the remembered route to the gravel road that led to the cabin Archie had shown them. Then she crept along the half mile stretch the caller had described, scanning the road as the trees and foliage thickened and the road narrowed.

When they rounded a sharp bend, a clearing came into view up ahead, with a cabin nestled in the back part of it. A van was partially visible beside it.

Erin slowed the car to a crawl. When Miles hopped out and slammed the passenger door shut, she resumed a bit of speed, but not much. Hands clenched on the wheel as she watched him run into the trees ahead, her muscles tensed in fearful anticipation. Glancing in the rearview mirror, she saw the police car pull off the road out of sight.

Please, Lord, she prayed silently. *Control this situation. Protect my mother.*

When she pulled to a stop at the edge of the big yard, she took her time emerging from the car. Then she began a cautious approach, her heartbeat erratic and pounding harder with every step. When she reached the door, she paused to gather her courage.

Before she could knock, it swung open. She gasped. The man who peered out at her sported a face that hadn't seen a shaver in three or four days, and the coldest black eyes she had ever seen. And he gripped a gun in his hand. Behind her eyes, a vision formed of that face wearing a wig. He was the killer, she was sure of it. Deadly. And the fact that he hadn't bothered to cover that face meant he had no intention of letting her live.

"Get in here," he snarled.

"Release my mother. Then I'll come in." She backed away a step. "Where is she?"

"Erin! Is that you? Are you alright?" The shout came from inside the cabin.

"She's just fine," the man she knew as Mark Hammond from the pictures Miles had shown her yelled back at her. "But she won't be for long if she doesn't get in here."

"Don't listen to him, Erin," her mother shouted. "He'll just kill both of us if you come in here. Run!"

Hammond raised the gun. "Do as I said or you'll go first."

Panic seized Erin. She had no doubt he would kill her. He only wanted her inside so he could do it behind closed doors.

Where was Miles?

Had he made it to where he could get inside?

Was he waiting for the right moment?

Was Mom restrained? That had to be why she hadn't come to the door.

Lord, please spare my mother.

Mark Hammond reached out and grabbed her arm. Then he yanked her over the threshold. "I told you to get in here."

Inside the room, Erin spied Verna, seated in a straight-backed chair and bound to it with a strong cord around her waist. Mark apparently didn't see her as a threat, since she was blind. He didn't realize how keenly honed Mom's other senses were.

Erin shoved at him, jabbing her elbow into his ribs.

He grunted and cursed. Then his arm went around her neck. "You just earned this bullet," he said, raising the gun to her head.

She did the only thing she could think to do. She went limp and slumped against him.

The sudden shift of her falling dead weight made him stumble. As he did, the deafening crack of gunfire pierced the air, accompanied by her mother's scream and the shattering of glass that flew from the front window.

Suddenly there was a crash, and Miles burst through the back door, his gun drawn. Mark whirled, and a second shot exploded. His gun clattered to the floor, blood spattering from his hand. He screeched in pain, grabbed the hand with his good one and charged at Miles. They landed in a heap on the floor.

As Miles wrestled to an advantage and knelt over Mark, the two deputies rushed inside the cabin. They checked the fallen killer, and then yanked him to his feet. One deputy snapped a cuff on the uninjured wrist and hesitated about the bloody one. His partner grabbed that arm.

Erin closed her eyes for a second to draw a deep breath of relief. Then she ran to her mother, dropped to her knees and began to untie her.

When she finished, Miles crossed the room and scooped Erin into a fierce hug. She automatically turned into the embrace, welcoming the sweet haven of his arms. His head had begun a downward movement when a shout brought them up short.

"Stop!" Verna repeated as the deputies began to steer Mark Hammond toward the doorway. "He's only the hit man. His boss is in there."

She pointed toward the doorway of the second room of the cabin. "They think because I'm blind that I can't hear or smell. They were in the other room, but I heard him giving this one orders." She made a head motion toward Mark. "And I recognized his cologne from that political rally and meeting him at the mall."

Miles had his gun raised. One of the deputies took full charge of the prisoner, and his partner joined Miles, his gun also poised for action.

They moved to that door, one on either side, and Miles shouted, "Come out with your hands in the air."

When no one emerged, Miles reached for the knob and pushed the door open an inch. Then he gave it a hard kick. And they entered the room fast, Miles in the lead.

All Erin heard was silence for a couple of minutes. Then there were sounds of a scuffle. Moments later, they emerged, prodding Senator Fielder in front of them.

"Hiding in the closet like a kid—and the coward he is," the deputy said in disgust. He looked over at Verna. "Ma'am, will you testify against these two?"

"Of course, I will," she said, as if anyone would doubt it. "But right now I want someone to hand me a phone so I can call my husband and tell him the bad guys lost."

She reached out a hand, causing some amused looks. Erin gave her a phone.

~

Miles didn't sleep that night. He kept replaying how close he had come to losing Erin—and the fact that she had never been his to lose.

Pain twisted in his heart at imagining how big a hole he would have in his life when he left here. It would be on the scale of losing Shelly. And he couldn't go through that again.

Even if Erin wanted him to stay, he couldn't. She needed someone who would stay in one place. His job required travel and periods of time away from home. And she had made it clear that her work was her priority. Too many things stood in their way. Too many complications.

Leaving would be best for them both—and one of the hardest things he had ever done.

But he couldn't just disappear without saying goodbye.

He spent the weekend tying up loose ends of the case and preparing to leave town. The size and scope of the operation had surely taken years to build, with branches in other cities.

Monday, shortly before time for Erin's workday to end, he left the police station, drove to the mall and headed to her office. He found her standing in front of her door, locking it.

When he walked up behind her, she spun around in surprise. "Whoa," she said when she recognized him.

The sight of her knocked the wind out of him as he gripped her arm to steady her. The thought of life without her made him ache. "How are you?"

She peered at him through narrowed eyes. "I've had a long, hard day, as I'm sure you have. In addition to a full schedule, I've worked in some interviews."

"You're looking for a new office assistant?"

She nodded. "The employment agency is sending candidates."

"But you haven't found anyone suitable yet," he guessed.

She nodded, frowning. "Why are you here?"

"I wanted to be sure you're all right."

"I'm fine."

"I hope you aren't blaming yourself for anything. You were simply in the wrong place at the wrong time and got drawn into something dangerous that never should have happened to you—or your mother."

She drew a deep breath, hitching her purse strap onto her shoulder. "The one good thing that came from all of it, according to her, is that I met you. She likes you."

"I like her, too. I also like you." *I love you, but I can't stay.*

An awkward silence fell between them.

"I have to go," he said, stepping closer, uncaring if anyone happened to notice. "I already have a new assignment."

Then, against his better judgment, he pulled her to him and bent his head. Her lips came to meet his in a heart melting kiss that made it torture to let her go. But he did what he had to do.

She stepped back. "I wish you success. Please stay safe."

It took every bit of strength he could muster, but he mouthed a weak, "Goodbye," and walked away, leaving his heart behind.

Chapter 20

Erin flexed her back muscles, tired from a long day at the clinic operated at a rural Jamaican church. The mission team had done free eye exams, performed dozens of laser surgeries and delivered prescription glasses to children and elderly in this poor area over the past week.

Jamaica was a land of extremes—wealth on the northern coast and suburbs of Kingston, to poverty and squalor not far away—that made her more aware of the many blessings of her own home and life.

She had so much. Seeing these people and how they lived made her debts seem insignificant. She had the means and skills to eliminate them. Her parents needed her, yes, but not round the clock. They still functioned reasonably well on their own and valued their independence. She could look after them without smothering them.

Dad would tell her that worrying was futile, to leave everything in God's hands. Mom would say just do what you can and ask for help when it gets to be too much.

Erin knew they were right and tried to follow their advice. Yet there was a void in her life.

Miles.

His face came to her in the middle of the night. During the day. It floated in her mind now. She had wept when a birthday card arrived last week from him. She hadn't even realized he knew when her birthday was.

She wanted to call him. Tell him how much she loved him. Ask him to come back to her. Take her with him. But she couldn't do that. Only he could make that kind of decision.

She understood his fears. He was afraid to make another lifelong commitment and have it end prematurely.

Be with him, Lord. Heal him.

Knowing he was in God's hands, she drank the last of her coffee and returned to work.

~

Miles entered his St. Louis apartment, physically and mentally drained. He was also lonely, but God had become his confidant and source of strength. It had been nearly two months since he had returned and launched immediately into a new case. Once it had been concluded, he had gone to visit his parents, having forgiven them for giving him such a hard time over his decision to marry Shelly. During the past three days he had managed to reestablish a measure of rapport with them.

Now he had to deal with himself. Having just returned home, he was dogged by restlessness. And indecision.

He called in a pizza order and then took a quick shower before it was delivered. As he ate, questions bombarded him.

Had he done the right thing when he walked away from Erin rather than taking a chance—not telling her he loved her?

Now he searched his heart. He loved Erin, but was he willing to do whatever it took to be with her? Could he live without her? Did he want to?

She admitted that she gave her job priority. He had done the same.

A truth penetrated. There was more to life than just going to a job every day. Maybe both of them had lost sight of that.

The pain of losing Shelly still weighed on his heart. It always would. But healing was happening. He would always mourn her loss, but words she had said to him before her death came back to him. She had told him to mourn her for a while and then to move on with his life.

By the time he finished eating, he knew Shelly had been right. It was time to move on.

With Erin. If she'd have him.

He needed to talk to his boss first thing in the morning.

~

Erin gazed at the darkening sky out the window of the plane as it lowered over the Branson airport. The town being home to half of her team, it was where they had convened and begun their trip. When the plane had rolled to a stop on the runway, she removed her carry-on bag from above the seat and exited with the other mission team members.

When she entered the airport, she scanned faces, looking for Ginger, who had brought her down here for departure and was to pick her up and take her home. She followed the crowd to the baggage claim area, still not spotting Ginger. She located her bag and had just pulled it off the carousel when movement to her left made her turn. When she did, she gasped at the sight of Miles, looking so breathtakingly handsome in neat khaki slacks and a white polo shirt that it knocked the breath right out of her.

Was he really here? She reached out and touched the back of his hand. Yes, it was really him—not just a dream.

"What are you doing here?"

He gave her a lopsided, fake leer. "I'm kidnapping a doctor."

She laughed, feeling slightly giddy. "Does that mean you're my ride instead of Ginger?"

"Yep." He gripped the handle of her huge wheeled bag. "I'm parked right outside."

That meant he had talked to Ginger, who had a propensity for matchmaking.

Erin released her hold on the bag handle to let Miles take it and usher her out of the airport into the warm September evening. He quickly stowed her bag in the back seat of his truck and gave her a boost into the passenger seat.

"Am I correct in assuming you found a replacement assistant?" he asked as he drove out of the parking lot.

He seemed to be making chit chat, but she welcomed it. "Yes. And I've had a thorough background check done on her. She's an older woman, in her fifties, with years of experience. She's good with the patients. We get along great."

He pulled onto the highway. "I'm glad. I've learned a bit more about Lydia. She grew up in the same neighborhood as Ray Fielder, and she knew his cousin Leland Zink from visits with the Zink family. She learned her way around the campaign trail and men—the senator in particular—at a young age."

"So she and Fielder had a relationship that dates back to around the time he became a senator, or maybe before," Erin theorized.

Miles nodded. "She admits that it started when she was still in her teens and continued over the years, even though he got married. And here's one more interesting tidbit that has come to light. Fielder was driving the motorcycle that hit a car, killing the driver, when he and Leland were juveniles. His rich parents got the case buried to keep his record clean."

"It's hard to believe what people will do for money and power. Greed is a horrible thing. But I have one good thing to report," she said, shaking off the melancholy caused by the thoughts. "Freddy has a girlfriend. It's someone who works with him at the food mart. I met them in the hallway one day, and he introduced her to me."

Miles smiled. "I'm happy for him."

Erin's attention returned suddenly to the here and now, trying to hide her confusion. She was thrilled that Miles was here. But why had he come?

"Where are you taking me?" she asked when he turned toward historic downtown rather than heading north.

"Somewhere we can talk."

Nervous flutters bounced in her stomach as he pulled into a parking lot, slipped his hand over hers and led her up Branson Landing, a mile and a half of Taneycomo Lakefront boardwalk. She remembered mentioning to him that this waterfront shopping area was a favorite spot of hers. Located within walking distance of the tourism district, it contained a convention center, tourism center, marina, hotels, condominiums and penthouses.

At the heart of the landing, benches on each terraced level of the town square provided seating where visitors could rest and watch the hourly water show. At a vacant bench on the upper level, Miles tugged her down beside him. Then he draped an arm along the top of the bench behind her shoulders.

As he faced her in the glow of the lights, Erin saw a tentative look cross his face. She didn't know what to think.

He lifted her chin with the tip of a finger. "Your friend Ginger isn't the only person I've spoken to," he said, his eyes moving over her in solemn scrutiny, as if trying to read her mind.

"Oh?" She couldn't decipher his tone.

"I made a mistake when I left here. I hope you're glad I'm back."

The uncertainty in his eyes tugged at her heart. She drew a deep breath and put it all on the line. "I'm more than glad. I've missed you terribly, wished and prayed every day— even while in Jamaica—to see you again, be with you. I love you so much."

The admission felt bold, but it was honest.

A slow smile covered his handsome face. "I've been to see your parents, and they've given me their blessing and permission to ask you to marry me. I love you and want nothing more than to spend the rest of my life with you. Will you marry me?"

Afraid the euphoria she felt would lift her right up off the ground, Erin leaned forward as he dipped his head. His kiss was tender and warm. Heavenly.

When he pulled away, she kept her arms around him. "I'll marry you, live wherever you need to live."

"Your parents say they're thinking of selling their home and moving into senior housing, and they want to live near us, no matter where that is."

"How do you feel about that?"

"It makes me happy." The look on his face was too joyous to be forced. Knowing he felt that way about her parents made everything that much better.

With love overflowing in her heart, Erin went back into his arms.

Overhead speakers erupted into loud music, and the fountains began a spectacular display of water, fire and light, one-hundred-foot shooting geysers and blasting fire cannons, all choreographed to lights and music.

It all went unnoticed as he kissed her again.

***

Can Officer Jonathan Zalinski
stop whoever is trying to harm
Ginger Brewer before it's too late?
Find out in *Crime of Conveyance*,
Book Two of this series,
Coming in a few weeks.

BOOKS by Helen Gray

ROMANCES
Ozark Sweetheart
Ozark Reunion
Ozark Wedding

Bandit Bride
Prairie Bride

Bootheel Bride
Bootheel Bachelor
Bootheel Betrothal

Show Me Love
Heartland Illusions
Mozark Vision
Missouri Catch

Schoolhouse Justice
Small Town Injustice
Workplace Danger

Paige's Proposal
Brooke's Bargain
Haley's Hero
Kelsey's Keeper

NOVELLAS
River Town Romance
(2 in 1, Hawthorn Hope &
Tree of Hope)

Love Blooms
(2 in 1, Pasque Plight &
Black-Eyed Susan's Secret)

Mother Road Matches
(2 in 1, Shamrock Ruby &
Dream Team)

Secrets in the Park

Gift Bride (Sequel to Dodge
City Duos)

A Time to Love

MYSTERIES
Educated in Murder
Preyed in Murder
Coached in Murder
Rivaled in Murder
Keyed in Murder
Tutored in Murder